The Fiend with Twenty Faces

Edogawa Rampo

The Fiend with Twenty Faces

Edogawa Rampo

Translated
by
Dan Luffey

with illustrations by
Tim Smith 3

Kurodahan Press
2012

The Fiend with Twenty Faces by Edogawa Rampo
Translated by Dan Luffey

Original copyright Hirai Kentarō.
English translation copyright © 2012 Dan Luffey.

FG-JP0027-A2
ISBN: 978-4-902075-36-6

KURODAHAN PRESS
www.kurodahan.com

Contents

Continued

Preface

Ho-Ling Wong

You could walk into any Tokyo neighborhood and witness the same peculiar occurrence: whenever people started to talk together, they would begin with rumors about the fiend known as "Twenty Faces."

Generations of Japanese readers have grown up reading these famous opening lines of *The Fiend With Twenty Faces* (1936), the first novel in the *Boy Detectives* children's mystery series written by Edogawa Rampo (*nom de plume* of Hirai Tarō, 1894–1965). The *Boy Detectives* series, numbering more than two dozen volumes, chronicles the confrontations between master detective Akechi Kogorō and his assistants the Boy Detectives and dastardly criminals—especially Twenty Faces. Said to have been read by more than a hundred million readers, it is still in print in Japan (Sunada 2009, 240). The enduring popularity of the series can also be seen in its influence on popular culture, which at times has taken morbid forms. Who, for example, could forget the infamous Glico-Morinaga Case of 1984 in which a gang of criminals kidnapped the president of confectioner Ezaki-Glico and, after the president's escape, started to blackmail various food manufacturers? The criminals called themselves Twenty-One Faces, in a grim nod to Rampo's master criminal.

Readers of Rampo's work are probably familiar with his *ero-guro* (erotic grotesque) nonsense work, stories of the bizarre and grotesque, of the sensual and shocking. From stories that tell about a man who derives pleasure from spying on people in *Yaneura no Sanposha* (*The Stalker in the Attic*, 1925) to a man who lives inside a chair in *Ningen Isu* (*The Human Chair*, 1925), Rampo's work captivates readers precisely *because* it is unsettling. And indeed, most translations of Rampo's work up until now have focused on this part of his literary output. However, one should never forget that Rampo is also known for his Boy Detectives children's series. In fact, most people in Japan nowadays probably first learned about Rampo when they read a Boy Detectives novel at school. I was pleasantly surprised when I visited a middle school in Fukuoka, Japan, in 2010 and saw that the Boy Detectives novels were kept in a special display in the school library. The book you hold in your hands now is thus the book that has led many generations of readers to Rampo-mania and will probably continue doing so until the end of time.

THE ORIGIN OF THE BOY DETECTIVES

The fictional master detective Akechi Kogorō had been used by Rampo in several earlier stories such as *D-Zaka Satsujin Jiken* (*Case of the Murder at D-Slope*, 1925) and *Shinri Shiken* (*The Psychological Test*, 1925), but in the Boy Detectives series, he is helped by his young assistant Kobayashi Yoshio and the titular Boy Detectives, a gang of children. Their nemesis is Twenty Faces, a mysterious thief who derives his name from the fact that he is a master of disguise. *The Fiend with Twenty Faces* chronicles the first confrontation between Akechi, Kobayashi and Twenty Faces, with the Boy Detectives organization being set up halfway through the story.

The main inspiration for *The Fiend with Twenty Faces* was clearly the Arsène Lupin series written by Maurice Leblanc (1864-1941). Twenty Faces not only shares a knack for disguise with the (in)famous gentleman-burglar, but they both have a peculiar dislike for blood and choose to commit their crimes without resorting to violence, instead relying on cunning. Both Lupin and Twenty Faces also have the habit of announcing their crimes in advance, basically challenging the police to try to stop them. *The Fiend with Twenty Faces* was actually originally conceived as a story featuring a young Lupin as the protagonist before it was changed to its final form (Togawa 2003, 94).

The Arsène Lupin series also provided Rampo with an example of how a confrontation between a master detective and a master criminal would unfold. Maurice LeBlanc had already let Arsène Lupin meet with a thinly disguised Sherlock Holmes in *Sherlock Holmes Arrives Too Late* (1907) and *Arsène Lupin versus Holmlock Shears* (1908) and the influence these classic stories had on Rampo can also be seen in *Kurotokage* (*The Black Lizard*, 1934), where Akechi Kogorō is confronted with the female master criminal The Black Lizard. In this sense, *The Fiend with Twenty Faces* can be viewed as a more child-friendly version of *The Black Lizard*.

The final important influence the *Arsène Lupin* series had on Rampo's Boy Detectives series is apparent in the creation of Akechi's assistant Kobayashi Yoshio. Even though Kobayashi is a ten-year-old boy, he is recognized as a talented detective capable of holding his own in a battle of wits against Twenty Faces. The situation of a young detective versus a master criminal mirrors the way in which young detective Isidore Beautrelet manages to work against Arsène Lupin in *The Hollow Needle* (1909), one of Lupin's greatest adventures. Isidore Beautrelet himself brings to mind Joseph Rouletabille, the young reporter-detective who first appeared in Gaston Leroux's *The Mystery of the Yellow Room* (1907). Kobayashi can thus be considered a direct descendant of these young French detectives.

The image of the great detective Akechi being assisted by a gang of children naturally evokes Sherlock Holmes and the Baker Street Irregulars, a group of street urchins who were Holmes's eyes and ears in London. However, it must be stressed that the Boy Detectives are definitely more than just the eyes and ears of Akechi: they are real detectives who seek out actual cases and try to solve them themselves. From kidnapping to theft, if it is a crime, they will fight it. Akechi only intervenes when things get too dangerous for children. This plot device, whereby children are the protagonists in a mystery story but are backed up by adult characters, is still common in modern Japanese mystery comics and cartoons. It is no exaggeration to state that Rampo's Boy Detectives series shaped contemporary Japanese juvenile mystery fiction.

The Birth of the Boy Detectives

The Fiend with Twenty Faces was originally serialized from January to December 1936 in the children's magazine *Shōnen Kurabu* (Boys' Club). At first glance, the combination of *Shōnen Kurabu* and Rampo is an odd one. *Shōnen Kurabu* was one of the most popular "boys adventure" magazines. These were basically educational magazines whose goal was to foster upstanding citizens through a variety of children's fiction with a nationalistic tone. The magazine also included "coming-of-age" stories, tips on studying, and information about upcoming school entrance exams (Maeda 2004, 211). Rampo, on the other hand, was famous for his *ero-guro* nonsense stories like *The Stalker in the Attic, The Human Chair,* and *Injū* (*Beast in the Shadows*, 1928), which captivated the hearts of his adult audience with erotic and grotesque horror. In fact, few writers could have been *further* from *Shōnen Kurabu*'s educational ideal than Rampo. But, as with most things in this world, the basic elements of market economics, supply and demand, managed to even out these differences.

On the demand side, *Shōnen Kurabu* had been looking for new kinds of stories to publish. For years, it had been putting out mystery serials featuring child detectives as the protagonists. While those series were certainly popular with readers, the editors at *Shōnen Kurabu* were dissatisfied with them. Sherlock Holmes possessed a wide variety of talents that allowed him to fight crime and was a hero for children to look up to. But child protagonists with the same talents were unconvincing, so the stories felt unrealistic and lacked a feeling of suspense (Maeda 2004, 210). The editors felt they needed to get rid of the Superman-like child protagonist in order to heighten the suspense.

In 1935 the editors of *Shōnen Kurabu* decided to ask Rampo to write a children's mystery for them. It must not have been an easy choice. Rampo's fictional master detective Akechi Kogorō was certainly precisely what they had been looking for: an adult master detective who would be able to bring back the suspense in their mystery stories. Rampo, however, was not a writer people associated with the educational role *Shōnen Kurabu* was so proud of. His *ero-guro* nonsense stories were clearly not fit for the magazine. It was also an era in which several crimes in the news were linked to Rampo's stories. There was, for example, a thief, who entered a neighboring house through the loft, as in Rampo's *The Stalker in the Attic*. In another case Rampo's name was linked to a boy who sneaked into a school, because he had a copy of Rampo's *Issun Bōshi* (*The Dwarf,* 1926) on him. It was a bold move by the editors of *Shōnen Kurabu* to approach a writer like Rampo to write a story for them (Togawa 2003, 81).

While it certainly came as a surprise to Rampo, the request by *Shōnen Kurabu* to write a children's mystery story came at a most fortuitous time for him. The 1930s were an era of growing imperialism in Japan, and Rampo had been suffering military censorship for several years. The most famous example is that of his short story *Imomushi* (*The Caterpillar,* 1929), which describes the life of a poor soldier who has lost his arms and legs in war and must be taken care of by his wife. The anti-militaristic tone of the story was deemed unfit by the authorities, and the story was first rewritten to comply with censorship standards. As Japanese society moved towards the Pacific War, however, *The Caterpillar* was completely cen-

sored (Matsuyama 1990, 248). With freedom and individuality compromised in this militarized society, Rampo had been
in a writing slump for years, having lost his creative drive,
and as a result he was receiving fewer and fewer requests for
manuscripts. He thus happily accepted *Shōnen Kurabu*'s offer.
Interestingly, Rampo also noted that he had always felt that his
stories, although intended for adults, had a rather childish side
to them, and he thus felt that writing for children would not
be much different from his usual writing (Togawa 2003, 82).

The Fiend with Twenty Faces turned out to be a hit, but
the writing process was not an easy one for Rampo. Just one
month after the start of the serialization of *The Fiend with
Twenty Faces* Japanese society was shocked by the infamous
February 26 Incident, an attempted coup d'état carried out by
troops of the Imperial Japanese Army, which resulted in the
murders of several high-ranking politicians, including Saitō
Makoto, Lord Keeper of the Privy Seal of Japan, and Minister
of Finance Takahashi Korekiyo. The revolt was suppressed in
three days but led to the tightening of militaristic rule. For
Rampo it meant that he also had to keep military censorship
in mind as he wrote *The Fiend with Twenty Faces*. In fact, Rampo originally planned to use Twenty Faces as the protagonist
of the story, but it was not possible to use a *criminal* as the
protagonist. He had also planned to title his story *Kaitō Nijū
Mensō* (Mysterious Thief with Twenty Faces) as a nod to Arsène Lupin (known as *Kaitō Rupan* in Japan), but he was told
that he was not allowed to use the Chinese character *tō* (盗;
to steal, thief). The interference of the military only grew as
Japan moved towards war, and by the time Rampo wrote *Yōkai
Hakase* (1938), the third volume in the Boy Detectives series,
he was no longer allowed to depict criminal actions in his stories at all (Washitani 2000, 73).

Despite these hurdles, however, the publication of *The
Fiend with Twenty Faces* turned out to be a win-win situation

for everyone. *Shōnen Kurabu* got a hit story. Rampo got over his writing slump. And the readers got a great adventure.

THE LIFE OF THE BOY DETECTIVES

If one considers that most readers of *Shōnen Kurabu* were children from the upper middle classes, then the success of *The Fiend with Twenty Faces* is not surprising. These readers were children who had their own private study rooms, who had to cram for entrance exams, and whose parents expected them to get prestigious jobs. In short, they were to be the future elite. The adventures of Akechi, Kobayashi and the Boy Detectives provided a great way for these children to escape from the reality of "entrance exam hell" and the dreariness of ordinary life. The stories were also very recognizable to them, with many points in common with their own lives to draw them in. For example, the concept of the Boy Detectives, a group of young boys working together to fight crime, mirrored the numerous Boy Scout-like *Gakkō Shōnendan* organizations. These school organizations, often with a nationalistic educational tone, were meant to involve children in after-school activities (Maeda 2004, 212). How enticing it must have been to read these stories about going on adventures in a group while taking a break from study. It is also no coincidence that the enemy of the Boy Detectives is Twenty Faces, who is not only a thief and kidnapper but also someone who often disguises himself as a homeless man or idle musician, basically a personification of everything the authorities deemed a menace to society.

The Boy Detectives stories also formed a fictional world in which children learned to cope with the development of Japan. Tokyo had rapidly urbanized and modernized, especially after the Great Kantō Earthquake in 1923, and children were growing up in big grey concrete city blocks. Prior to that time, children had grown up playing outside. They saw their parents doing small-scale manufacturing work in their homes and knew all their neighbors. By the 1930s, however, parents were working outside the home, and ties with neighbors had weakened. The concrete city had become an unknown and menacing place for children. The scene in *Yōkai Hakase* in which the Boy Detective Taiji gets lost while following a suspicious man would have been very familiar to the readers. It was also in this city, this grey asphalt maze, where the urban legend of *Akai Manto* (The Red Cape) was born in the 1930s. *Akai Manto,* a monster who kidnapped and murdered young girls, is said to have been based on an actual murder of a young girl in Tokyo and a *kamishibai* (a form of storytelling using storyboard illustrations) called *Akai Manto* (Matsuyama 1999, 252). The rumors surrounding Akai Manto struck fear into the hearts of children, and the character of Twenty Faces, as an unknown, mysterious criminal, naturally invoked this fear, especially when in later Boy Detectives novels Twenty Faces actually began to kidnap children more frequently. The way the Boy Detectives bravely choose to fight against the master criminal must have been a source of encouragement for many readers. The stories taught them to be courageous, to stand up against crime, and that teamwork would solve everything.

The adventures of the Boy Detectives were thus both friend and teacher to their readers. The following passage in *The Fiend with Twenty Faces* in which Sōji explains the Boy Detectives to Kobayashi sums it up best:

"We're going to create an association called the Boy Detectives. Of course, we're going to do it so that it won't interfere with our schoolwork. My dad also said that it's OK as long as it doesn't get in the way of school."

The Boy Detectives stories allowed children to take a break from their busy study schedule, but the stories were ultimately considered nothing more than a brief interlude on their way to becoming fruitful members of society.

THE LEGACY OF THE BOY DETECTIVES

Rampo managed to write only three Boy Detectives novels before the outbreak of the Pacific War, but returned with new energy after the war. In fact, writing the Boy Detectives series became Rampo's main source of income after the war, as he stopped writing stories aimed at adults and concentrated exclusively on writing the Boy Detectives series and critiques of detective fiction.

The popularity of the series grew explosively in the postwar years, and it did not take long to become a real multimedia mammoth. Following the radio drama *Rampo to Seidō no Majin* (*Rampo and the Bronze Devil*) in 1952, the Boy Detectives began to be seen everywhere. Their first film appearance was in 1954, and their first TV appearance in 1958 (Sakurai 2007, 74-75). Since then, the Boy Detectives have been seen in countless TV shows and movies. The postwar Boy Detectives were definitely more commercialized and, befitting media geared for children, the series spawned a wide range of merchandise, from notebooks to replicas of the so-called BD badges, which provided proof of membership in the Boy Detectives. Most recently the Boy Detectives appeared in the 2008 action film "K-20," which tells an original story with Twenty Faces, Akechi and Kobayashi based on a novel by Kitamura Sō.

Twenty Faces, Akechi and the Boy Detectives are still household names in Japan, and the adventures of the Boy Detectives live on in the form of modern Japanese comics. The detective comic is a popular genre in Japan, with series like *Tantei Gakuen Q* (*Detective Academy Q*) and *Kindaichi Shōnen no Jikenbo* (*The Kindaichi Case Files*) all featuring young detectives with master criminals as their nemeses. The influence of the Boy Detectives series and Rampo in general is most apparent in the hit comic series *Meitantei Konan* (*Detective Conan*), which features a 16-year-old detective who gets turned into a small boy and adopts the alias Edogawa Conan. Conan also has his own gang of children called the *Detective Boys* who help him solve cases, and even the gadgets Conan utilizes mirror the seven detective tools Kobayashi carries on him.

The cityscape of Tokyo, the political environment, even the way in which people first learn about the Boy Detectives, may have changed in the past 75 years. But you can still walk into any Tokyo neighborhood and hear the names of Twenty Faces, Akechi Kogorō and the Boy Detectives being mentioned. Some things will never change.

BIBLIOGRAPHY

Maeda Kazuo 前田一男. "Kyōiku ni Senpuku suru Shōnen Tantei Dan" (The Boy Detectives Hidden in Education) 公教育に潜伏する 少年探偵団. In *Edogawa Rampo to Taishū Nijūseiki* (Edogawa Rampo and the Mass Culture of the 20th Century) 江戸川乱歩と大衆の二十世紀, ed. Fujii Hidetata 藤井淑禎, pp. 208-215. Tokyo: Shibundō, 2005.

Matsuyama Iwao 松山巌. *Rampo to Tokyo: 1920 Toshi no Katachi* (Rampo and Tokyo: The Form of the City in 1920) 乱歩と東京１９２０都市の貌. Tokyo: Futabasha, 1999.

Sakurai Yoshito 桜井由人. "Terebi, Eiga no Shōnen Tantei Dan" (The Boy Detectives of TV and Movies) テレビ・映画の少年探偵団. In *Bokutachi no Daisuki na Akechi Kogorō* (The Akechi Kogorō We Really Love) 僕たちの大好きな明智小五郎, ed. Satō Fumiaki佐藤文照, pp. 74-75. Tokyo: Takarajimasha, 2007.

Sunada Hiroshi 砂田弘. "Shōnen Tantei Shirīzu no Makuake – Kaijin Nijū Mensō to Akechi Kogorō no Taiketsu" (The Start of the Boy Detectives Series – The Confrontation between The Fiend with Twenty Faces and Akechi Kogorō)「少年探偵」シリーズの幕あけ―怪人二十面相と明智小五郎の対決. Commentary to: Edogawa Rampo 江戸川乱歩. *Kaijin Nijū Mensō* (The Fiend with Twenty Faces) 怪人二十面相. Tokyo: Poplar Publishing, 2005

Togawa Yasunobu 戸川安宣. "Rampo Shōnen Mono no Sekai" (The World of Rampo's Juvenile Fiction) 乱歩・少年ものの世界. In *Edogawa Rampo Wandārando Shinsōban* (Edogawa Rampo Wonderland – New Edition) 江戸川乱歩ワンダーランド 新装版, ed. Nakajima Kawatarō中島河太郎, pp. 81-99. Tokyo: Chūsekisha.

Washitani Hana 鷲谷花. "Kaijin, Teito wo Sekkensu: Kaijin Nijū Mensō to Shōnen Kurabu no Chiseigaku" (The Phantom Thief in the Imperial Capital: Kaijin 20 Mensō and the Topology of Shōnen-Club) 怪人、帝都を席巻す：『怪人二十面相』と『少年倶楽部』の地政学. *Daigaku Kenkyū Ronshū* 大学研究論集17 (2000), pp. 71-81.

The Fiend with
Twenty Faces

Edogawa Rampo

1 THE STAGE IS SET

YOU COULD WALK INTO any Tokyo neighborhood and witness the same, peculiar occurrence: whenever people started to talk together, they would begin with rumors about the fiend known as "Twenty Faces."

"Twenty Faces" was the nickname given to the mysterious thief who grabbed newspaper headlines daily. They said he possessed twenty different faces: a master of disguise.

No matter how well-lit the location or how closely he was watched, "Twenty Faces" could transform himself into a completely different person, leaving no sign he was disguised. Young and old, rich and poor, scholar and vagabond... why, he could even become a woman!

Nobody knew the villain's age, nor which of his faces was the real one. The myriad masks and disguises he donned were so different from one another, they said, that maybe even the villain himself had forgotten his true identity!

Twenty Faces' masterful disguises stumped even the police. They could hardly figure out which face to begin hunting for.

The one blessing was that he stole only rare and beautiful items such as art and jewelry. Twenty Faces seemed to have no interest in cash and had never injured or killed anyone. He hated blood.

Even so, he was still a criminal. If threatened there was no telling what he might do to escape, and that fear elicited the many rumors. The rich men and women of Japan with priceless and unique valuables were particularly paranoid. Everything they had heard so far proved this thief couldn't be stopped no matter how many times the police were called.

Twenty Faces had one peculiar habit: Once he selected his next target, he would always deliver a warning, announcing when he would come to get it. Perhaps he preferred to fight his battles on even ground, despite his thieving ways. Or maybe he was simply bragging that he always got the last laugh no matter how many people tried to stop him. Whatever the reason, everyone agreed this fiendish thief was one heck of an arrogant daredevil.

The account that is about to unfold, Intrepid Reader, chronicles the magnificent, one-on-one battle of wits between the greatest detective in Japan, Akechi Kogorō, and this inexplicably elusive thief.

Master detective Akechi Kogorō had an assistant named Kobayashi Yoshio, a little detective as nimble as a squirrel, and quite the sight to see.

Now that the stage is set, let us proceed to the main event.

2 A Steel Trap

AMONG THE AZABU DISTRICT estates of Tokyo sat a hundred-square-meter mansion. In front of it, a towering four-meter wall ran along the property as far as the eye could see. Stepping through the massive steel gate, one would spy a huge sago palm dominating the lawn, and, beyond its thick leaves, the elegant entryway. The spacious Japanese-style house stood at a right angle to a yellow brick two-story western-style home. Behind them stretched out a garden as beautiful and open as a public park.

This was the domain of Hashiba Sōtarō, a respected leader in the business world. And at this very moment, his family was both extremely happy—and terrified.

They were joyous because Sōichi, Mr. Hashiba's eldest son, was finally returning from Borneo to mend relations with his father. Sōichi was an adventurer by nature, and upon graduating from secondary school he had voyaged with two peers to a mysterious new land in the South Seas. Despite Sōichi's entreaties to be allowed to start some new and exciting enterprise, Mr. Hashiba vehemently refused to permit it. So, in the end, Sōichi simply ran away from home and hopped on a boat to the South Pacific.

Ten years passed, and Sōichi's family received not a single request for aid from their son nor a single clue to his whereabouts. Then three months ago they received an unexpected letter from Sandakan Village in Borneo, saying, "I've proved myself now and want to come home and apologize to Father."

Sōichi said he was running a rubber tree plantation in the
Sandakan area and included a photograph of himself at his

plantation. Now thirty years old, he sported a stylish mustache and looked to have become a fine, upstanding adult.

His parents, little sister Sanae, and ten-year-old brother Sōji, were overjoyed. Sōichi said he would fly home from the seaport of Shimonoseki.

And what about the fear gripping the Hashibas, you ask? The source of that, of course, was none other than the spine-tingling notice sent by Twenty Faces, which read,

> I am sure that even simple folk like yourselves have learned just who I am from the newspapers. Recently, I was told by reliable sources that you and your brood are in possession of six crown jewels from the late Romanov family, which you value as family treasures. For my next venture, I have decided to accept these six jewels from you, free of charge.
>
> I will be by to pick them up in the next few days. I will notify you of the exact time in due course. Please take all due precautions.

The letter was signed "Twenty Faces."

The diamonds the thief spoke of were indeed from the crown of the House of Romanov. After the February Revolution, the crown fell into the hands of a White Russian, who pried loose the jewels and sold them to a Chinese merchant. Over the years they passed through many hands until they were finally purchased by the Hashibas for the princely sum of two million yen.

The six jewels were now shut tight within a safe in Mr. Hashiba's study. Judging from the fiend's letter, however, he seemed to have already sniffed out their exact hiding spot.

As the master of the house, Mr. Hashiba kept his composure after reading the letter, but his wife and daughter shook with fear, as did the servants.

Kondō, the elderly steward of the Hashiba house, took immediate action. Deeming this a perilous danger for his employers, he went straight to the police and demanded protection, even going so far as to buy a savage dog to prepare in every possible way for the villain's attack.

A police officer lived near the Hashiba estate, and Kondō asked him to call his off-duty friends to insure there were always two or three policeman keeping a vigilant eye on the grounds.

Three brawny houseboys also lived on the estate. With the security of policemen, strong young men, and a fierce watch-dog, no one thought even a master thief like Twenty Faces would be able to make his way in.

All that was left now was to await Sōichi's return. Their eldest boy had left for the southern islands empty-handed ten years before but was returning a successful man. The family began to feel that as long as Sōichi returned home safely, they would have nothing more to worry about.

IT WAS EARLY MORNING on the day Sōichi was to arrive at Haneda Airport in Tokyo. Bright autumn sunlight shone down on the Hashibas' earthen storehouse, from which a young boy appeared. It was little Sōji. It was still too early for breakfast, so the grounds were blanketed in silence. Only the early-waking sparrows could be heard, chirping loudly from

the storehouse roof and tree branches in the garden. Clad in a toweling robe, Sōji was heading down the stone steps into the garden carrying an unusual metal contraption in his hands. What in the world was the little guy up to?

The night before he had had a frightening dream: Twenty Faces had crept into the study on the second floor of the western-style building and stolen the treasure! The thief's face was chillingly pale and expressionless, just like the Noh mask hanging in his father's room. After stealing the treasure, he quickly opened a window and jumped out into the garden.

Sōji awoke with a scream, but soon realized that it had only been a nightmare. For some reason, he felt it was a premonition. *That scoundrel Twenty Faces is gonna jump out the window, I know it! Then he's gonna cut across the garden and get away*, he thought. *There's a flowerbed right there, and that's where he'll land!*

As he continued to imagine the scene, a thought suddenly popped into Sōji's mind.

Oh boy, that's it! What a great idea. . . I'll set a trap in the flowerbed! If things go as I think they will, then the thief will try and cut across here for sure! But if I set a trap, I can catch him!

Sōji was planning to use an American steel trap, one a forester friend of his father's had brought over for a demonstration about a year ago. It had been shut away in the storehouse ever since, but Sōji still remembered it well.

The boy became obsessed with the idea. It was doubtful whether the thief would actually get caught in a lone trap set in such a spacious garden, but now was not the time for such worries. He just wanted to try and set a trap on his very own. Sōji woke earlier than he ever had before, sneaked into the storehouse, and laboriously hauled out the heavy steel device.

He remembered that exciting feeling he had felt once before when setting a mousetrap. This time, though, his opponent was not a mouse, but a man. And not just any man, but the unparalleled master thief, Twenty Faces! His excitement was ten, no, twenty times greater than before. Dragging the steel trap to the center of the flowerbed, Sōji mustered all his strength and pushed open its saw-toothed jaws. After setting it up, he covered it with dead leaves to conceal it.

If the thief stepped inside, the trap would snap shut just like the mousetrap had. Its teeth would crash together like the massive black jaws of a wild beast, clamping down on and devouring the thief's ankle. It would be horrible if anyone from the house were caught, but since the trap was smack dab in the center of the flowerbed, Sōji couldn't see why anyone other than the thief would go there.

That should do it. I wonder if it'll work? Oh boy, oh boy. If the thief gets trapped, it'd be perfect! Please, please make things go well! Sōji pressed his palms together and prayed before walking back into the house with a grin.

It was truly a trap only a child could come up with—but the intuition of children is not to be underestimated. Do keep Sōji's trap in the back of your mind, Intrepid Reader. You'll see just how big a part it eventually plays.

3   MAN OR DEVIL?

THAT AFTERNOON, THE HASHIBA family traveled *en masse* to Haneda airport to welcome Sōichi home. The Sōichi who stepped off the airplane was just as gallant and dashing as everyone had imagined. With a dark-brown coat over his arm, a smart business suit of the same color, and sharp creases in his trousers that made him appear tall and slender, he looked like a movie star from the West.

His dark-brown felt hat sheltered an attractive, smiling face with a coppery tan that matched his clothes. Sōichi had thick, straight eyebrows; big, shining eyes; and white, even teeth that shone when he smiled. The thin mustache lining his upper lip also seemed strangely familiar. He looked just as he had in the photograph. No—now that his family could see Sōichi in person, he looked even more splendid.

After shaking hands with everyone, Sōichi got into the car between his mother and father. Sōji rode in the following car with his sister and the steward, Kondō. The cars drove so closely together that Sōji was able to keep his eyes locked firmly on his older brother, hardly able to contain his joy.

Once home, everyone surrounded Sōichi and showered him with questions. Evening came before they knew it, and mother's home-made dinner awaited them in the dining room. The dining table was covered with a brand-new tablecloth. On the grand table was a beautiful autumn flower arrangement, sparkling silver knives and forks, and napkins folded and positioned fancily for the occasion.

Sōichi was the focus of the family's conversation throughout the meal. At every opportunity, he regaled them with tales of the exotic South Seas interspersed with anecdotes of his youth.

"Back then, Sōji, you barely knew how to walk, and were always charging into my study and rummaging through my desk. One time you knocked over a bottle of ink and rubbed it all over your hands and face. It looked like you had turned into a Negro! Remember all the commotion, Mother?"

While Sōichi's mother couldn't exactly recall whether or not such a thing had happened, she was so overcome with joy that tears came to her eyes as she nodded again and again.

And then, Intrepid Reader, a frightening development dispelled the joy of the Hashiba family cleanly and cruelly with the delicate finality of a violin string snapping.

What a cruel-hearted devil! The ten-year reunion of parents and son, brother and sister: it was during this once-in-a-lifetime celebration that his dreadful presence crept in, shattering the family's joy.

In the middle of another reminiscence, one of the houseboys brought in a telegram, and no matter how immersed they all were in their reminiscing, the telegram simply begged to be opened.

Mr. Hashiba knit his eyebrows, read the message and then fell unusually quiet.

"Father, is something wrong?" Sōichi's sharp eyes instantly discerned his father's distress.

"Hmm. Yes, a small problem has arisen. I don't want to worry you, but we will all have to be extremely careful tonight."

He showed them the telegram, which said: "TONIGHT AT THE STROKE OF 12, I WILL COME TO GET WHAT I SAID I WOULD." It was signed "20," which must have been an abbreviation for Twenty Faces, and the "stroke of 12" surely referred to midnight, when the thief would come to steal the diamonds.

"Could the '20' refer to that criminal known as Twenty Faces?" Sōichi stared at his father in surprise.

"Yes. I'm surprised you've heard of him, son."

"After disembarking at Shimonoseki, I heard various rumors about him and happened to read a newspaper article on the plane. So he's gotten around to our house. But what could he be after?"

"After you left home, I came into possession of a set of crown jewels—diamonds—from the late Russian tsar. That's what the thief wants."

Mr. Hashiba told his son all about Twenty Faces and the announcement. "Your presence is reassuring, but perhaps we should take turns guarding the jewels tonight."

"That sounds like a fine idea. I have confidence in my strength, and I'd love nothing more than to protect my family so soon after returning home."

Without delay, the estate was locked up tight under a vigilant guard. By the orders of the now pale-faced steward Kondō, all the gates were shut and locked from the inside, although it was only eight o'clock.

"Tonight, you must turn everyone away, no matter who comes to visit," he sternly ordered the servants.

Preparing to stay up all night, the three off-duty policemen, the three houseboys, and the family chauffeur split up the work, standing watch at the gates or patrolling the grounds. Mrs. Hashiba, Sanae, and Sōji were told to stay safe in their rooms with the doors locked. The numerous maids holed up in their sleeping quarters, nervously whispering to one another.

Meanwhile, Mr. Hashiba and Sōichi thief-proofed the study. Sandwiches and wine were laid out on a table as the men prepared to keep watch until morning.

The door and windows of the study were all locked and latched shut from the inside. Every access was tightly sealed, right down to the last termite's hole.

As he sat down in the study, Mr. Hashiba laughed nervously. "Maybe we overdid it a bit."

"There's no such thing as overdoing it against a villain like that. I've been reading up on Twenty Faces from the articles in the newspaper, and the more I read, the more frightening a fiend he seems." Sōichi's face was grim, and his voice revealed how uneasy he was.

"So you think the thief is still going to get inside despite all we've done so far?"

"Yes. It may sound like I'm frightened, but I have a very bad feeling."

"But how would he get in? To get to these jewels, he'd first have to climb those high gates. Then, even if he managed to hide himself from all the houseboys and sneak in, he'd still have to break this door down to get inside and *then* fight and defeat both of us. And that's not all! The jewels are inside this safe, which is impossible to open unless one knows the proper combination. No matter how much of a magician Twenty Faces may be, there's no way he could make it past all five of these obstacles." Mr. Hashiba laughed loudly. Behind his voice, however, an empty bravado resonated.

"But, Father, look. All of these articles talk about how the thief's performed absolutely impossible feats with ease, numerous times. There's even an example of someone who thought their belongings were fine because they were in a safe, but a hole was drilled in the back, and they were robbed unawares. There's another story here about a treasure that was guarded by five strong men. Somehow they ingested sleeping drugs without knowing it and ended up snoozing right through the crime. This man has the intelligence to come up with strategies to overcome any obstacle."

"Watch it, Sōichi, it almost sounds like you're praising him!" Mr. Hashiba stared at his son's face in surprise.

"No, this isn't praise. It's just the more I read about him, the more he scares me. His weapon isn't strength; it's intelligence. And if intelligence is used cleverly, the impossible is possible."

As father and son continued their discussion, the night deepened, and the wind began to blow. A black gust shot by, rattling the windows.

"You know, your excessive regard for this scoundrel has made me a little worried myself. I'm going to check on the jewels. If there were a hole in the back of the safe, it'd be disastrous."

Mr. Hashiba chuckled as he stood up and moved to the small safe in the corner of the room. He spun the dial and opened its door, removing a small, copper box. Embracing this precious item, he returned to his seat and placed it on the round table between himself and his son.

"This is the first time for me to see them." Sōichi's eyes glowed with curiosity as he spoke.

"Why, yes, I suppose it is. In that case, feast your eyes on the diamonds that once sparkled on the head of the tsar of Russia!"

He opened the box, revealing a blinding, prismatic glow. Six perfect bean-sized diamonds glittered on black velvet.

Mr. Hashiba waited until his son had gotten a good look, then closed the box. "I'm going to keep it here. It'll be safer to have it under our watch."

"Yes, I'm with you on that one."

The two soon ran out of things to talk about, resigning themselves to staring intently at that small box in the center of the table.

Sometimes, as if to remind them of its presence, the wind would blow by and rattle the windows. Far in the distance, a dog howled shrilly.

"It's almost time."

"It's 11:43. Seventeen more minutes." As Sōichi looked at his watch, the two became quiet again. Even the bold Mr. Hashiba's face was considerably paler, with sweat slightly beading on his forehead. Sōichi held clenched fists on his lap and gritted his teeth.

The room was so quiet that the slightest sound could be heard, from their breathing down to the ticking of Sōichi's watch, slicing away each second like a guillotine.

"How many minutes left?"

"Ten."

Just then they spied something tiny and white scurrying across the carpet. Was it a mouse?

Startled, Mr. Hashiba peered under the desk behind him where he had seen it run and hide.

"Oh, it's just a ping-pong ball. Where could it have come from, though?" After picking the ball up from under the desk, he studied it, confused.

"How odd. Maybe Sōji left it on one of the shelves over there and something knocked it down."

"You may be right. But what time is it?" The intervals between Mr. Hashiba's inquiries about the time had gradually become shorter and shorter.

"Four minutes left."

The two locked eyes. That second-slicing sound was now starting to frighten them.

Three, two, one. . . the appointed hour slowly approached. Perhaps Twenty Faces had already gotten over the wall. He could be walking through the hallways of the mansion as they spoke. Perhaps he was already outside the door, listening intently. *Ah. . . any moment now I'll hear a horrible sound, and he'll break the door down!*

"Father, is something wrong?"

"No, no, it's nothing. I will not let that Twenty Faces beat me!" Despite his words, Mr. Hashiba's face was already ghastly pale; both hands were pressed to his forehead.

Thirty. . . twenty. . . ten. . . Synchronized with their palpitations, suffocatingly terrifying seconds continued to pass.

"What's the time?" Mr. Hashiba's words sounded more like moans now.

"It's already 12:01."

"What, already one minute past? Hah! Look at that, Sōichi, Twenty Faces' pronouncement was wrong. The jewels are still right here. Not a single thing happened!" Mr. Hashiba let out a loud, triumphant laugh. But Sōichi didn't even smile.

"I can't believe it. Are you sure there's nothing wrong with the jewels? I doubt Twenty Faces is the kind of man who would break his word."

"What are you talking about? The jewels are right in front of you!"

"That's just a box."

"What, are you saying that there's nothing but a box here, and the diamonds have disappeared?"

"I want to be sure, Father."

Mr. Hashiba promptly stood up, gripping the copper box in his hands. Sōichi also rose. Their eyes met, and for a few moments they stared at each other, frozen.

"Let's open it, then. There's no way something that ridiculous could happen."

The lid of the box snapped open.

"Ah!"

They were gone. The black velvet was complete bare. It was as if the imperial diamonds had simply vanished into thin air!

4 THE MAGICIAN

FATHER AND SON DID nothing but silently stare at the other's blanched face.

Finally, Mr. Hashiba said with an irritated whisper, "This doesn't make sense!"

"No, it doesn't," Sōichi agreed. But strangely enough, Sōichi seemed not the least bit surprised or worried, and a vague smirk at the edge of his lips was visible.

"The door's still shut, and there's no way we wouldn't have seen someone come in here. He can't just pass through keyholes like a ghost, can he?"

"No, I doubt even Twenty Faces can transform himself into a ghost."

"Which means that the only people who could have gotten their hands on the diamonds are me—and you." Mr. Hashiba eyed his son suspiciously.

"That's right. You or me." Sōichi's smile grew until he was grinning.

"What's so funny?" Mr. Hashiba shouted as shock contorted his face.

"I'm impressed by this thief's skill. He's really something, you know. He kept his promise after all and charged straight through to his goal despite our meticulous preparations."

"That's enough! There you go, praising that crook again. You think getting outwitted by that scoundrel is funny?"

"Yes. In fact, your sheer panic is quite delightful to behold."

Is this the way a son should speak to his father? Rather than getting angry, Mr. Hashiba was merely dumbfounded. Then, for the first time, the smirking young man looked not like his son, but a complete stranger.

"Sōichi, don't move!" Aghast, Mr. Hashiba fixed his eyes on his son and moved to the buzzer on the wall.

"You are the one who mustn't move, Mr. Hashiba."

As odd as it may have seemed, Mr. Hashiba's own son had just called him Mr. Hashiba. Then, the man drew a small pistol from his pocket and aimed it straight at his own father. He was still grinning.

Seeing this, Mr. Hashiba froze.

"No calling for anyone now. And if you cry for help, I'll pull the trigger."

"Who are you? It can't be. . . ."

"Ha ha ha. So you finally realized, it seems. Relax, sir. I am not your son Sōichi, but the thief you call Twenty Faces, just as you guessed."

Mr. Hashiba stared at the man as if he were seeing a ghost—because there was still a mystery lurking in his mind that he just couldn't wrap his head around. If this was not his son, then who wrote that letter from Borneo? And who was really in that photograph?

"Twenty Faces is like the magicians in fairy tales. I can do what no one else can. Now, Mr. Hashiba, in exchange for those diamonds of yours, shall I explain the secret to my trick?"

Without a speck of worry in his voice, the eerie young man began calmly to explain.

"I began by doing research and discovering that your son Sōichi was missing. I also got my hands on a photograph of him before he left home. Then I simply imagined how dear Sōichi's face would have changed over the course of ten years, and, well, created the face you see now." The man poked his cheeks as he spoke. "The man in that photograph is none other than myself. I also wrote that letter, sent it with the photograph to a friend of mine in Borneo, and had him address it to you. Unfortunately, poor Sōichi's whereabouts are still unknown.

But he isn't in Borneo, that's for sure. You see, this was all just a theatrical performance by yours truly, from the very start."

Overcome with joy at their firstborn son's return, Mr. and Mrs. Hashiba never dreamed that it could all have been part of some atrocious plot.

"I'm a ninja," Twenty Faces boasted. "Do you see? Like that ping-pong ball. That's just one of my ninja weapons. I rolled it across the carpet myself, and then you bent under the desk to look for it. Taking the diamonds out from the box then was like taking candy from a baby. Ha ha ha. And now, sir, I bid you adieu."

Keeping his pistol trained on Mr. Hashiba, Twenty Faces stepped backwards and turned the door key with his left hand. The door opened, and he dashed into the hallway.

One window in the hall faced out on the garden. The thief unlatched it, opened it, and nimbly straddled its frame.

"Give this toy to little Sōji for me. I'm no killer," he said, tossing the pistol back into the room before leaping out the window.

Mr. Hashiba had been outwitted yet again. A toy! This child's plaything had kept him scared witless the entire time and prevented him from calling for anyone.

Now, Intrepid Reader, the key to this event is still fresh in your memory, isn't it? The window from which Twenty Faces jumped was the same one that appeared in little Sōji's dream. Beneath that window, Sōji's steel trap was waiting with its sharp teeth open wide. Sōji had seen the future, and there was a chance that his trap would come in handy, was there not? There was certainly a chance—and a very good chance at that!

5   IN THE LAKE

As soon as the thief discarded the pistol and jumped outside, Mr. Hashiba dashed to the window and looked down into
the dim garden. It was night, but lights illuminated the court-
yard enough so that a person couldn't move about unseen.

After the thief fell, he froze face down on the ground, but
soon scrambled to his feet and started off at a fierce pace.

Just as Sōji had planned, Twenty Faces ran across the flowerbed. After he had taken a few steps, a violent metal gnashing
sounded out, and the black shadow of the thief crumpled to
the ground.

"Anyone there? It's the thief! The thief! Get to the garden!"
Mr. Hashiba shouted.

If not for the trap, the nimble Twenty Faces would have escaped. Sōji's simple plan had been a success! While the thief
struggled to remove the trap, seven people came running from
all directions: the policemen, the houseboys, and the chauffeur.

Mr. Hashiba raced down the stairs. With his steward Kondō,
he shined a flashlight into the garden and went to release the
captured man.

Oddly, the guard dog John they had bought specifically for
this event had yet to appear. If John had the thief in his sights
now, there would be no need to worry.

By the time Twenty Faces got out of the trap and stood up,
pursuers armed with flashlights had him surrounded in a ten
meter radius. He ran like the night wind. No, to say he ran like

a bullet would probably be closer to the mark. He whooshed through one side of the circle, dashing deeper into the garden.

Do remember, Intrepid Reader, that this garden was as big as a park. There was an artificial hill, a lake, and even a grove of trees that could pass for a forest. As dark as it was, seven was a far less than adequate number of people for the task at hand. And where was John?!

The pursuers were desperate in their effort. The three policemen especially knew what they were doing when it came to a manhunt. Seeing the thief run into the bushes at the top of the hill, they encircled it and tried to corner him on the other side, forcing him into the hands of the other pursuers.

There was no way the thief could escape beyond the outer wall. The wall around the garden itself was four meters tall, so as long as he hadn't brought a ladder with him, it would be impossible to scale.

"Ah, here! Here's the thief!" One of the houseboys called from the bushes.

Flashlights converged from every direction, and the bushes became as bright as day. The thief had curled into a ball and was attempting to roll into the forest to the right.

"Don't let him get away! He's off the hill!"

The flashlights flickered beautifully under the big trees and across the rocks of the expansive garden. Twenty Faces was a fast sprinter, so despite having him in sight, his pursuers could never catch up to their prey.

As the chase continued, an urgent telephone call alerted nearby policemen, who soon came to surround the outside of the wall. Twenty Faces was a rat in a trap.

This pulse-pounding game of hide-and-seek continued for a bit longer on the grounds, until the pursuers finally lost sight of Twenty Faces.

The thief ran straight ahead. Weaving his way through the trees, he was visible for one instant only to disappear the next. Then, he vanished altogether.

Everyone shined their lights over all the trees in the vicinity, but Twenty Faces was nowhere to be seen.

The outer wall was being watched by the policemen. The storm shutters on both the Western and Japanese houses were down, and lights from inside flooded the garden. Mr. Hashiba, Kondō, and Sōji, as well as the maids, had all come out onto the lawn and were staring at the trap in the garden, so there was no way he could have run in that direction.

The thief had to be hiding somewhere in the garden, but the seven pursuers couldn't find him no matter how hard they searched. Perhaps Twenty Faces had made use of his ninja skills once more.

In the end, they decided to wait until dawn to search again. Strict guard was kept over the front and back gates as well as the wall, and the thief was trapped, so waiting until morning should have been a safe choice.

To support the policemen outside, all of the pursuers left the garden except for Matsuno, the chauffeur, who remained in the garden alone.

The grove of trees surrounded a wide lake. After being stationed there, Matsuno was walking along the bank when he suddenly noticed something strange. Shining his flashlight around, he could see many fallen leaves floating at the edge of the water. A single stick of bamboo amid them was trembling—and not because of the wind. There was not a ripple on the water, yet, curiously, this single piece of bamboo was shaking.

A strange idea popped into Matsuno's head that almost made him want to run and alert everyone. He didn't have that much confidence in it, though. It was simply too hard to believe.

Shining his light on the bamboo, Matsuno bent down on the bank. Then, in order to confirm his suspicion, he searched through his pockets, pulled out a tissue, tore off a piece and placed it atop the bamboo. When he did, something truly unusual happened. The tissue began to float up and down over the hole in the bamboo. Clearly there was air going in and out.

It seemed impossible, and it was hard for Matsuno to accept what he thought was going on, but the proof was undeniable. Bamboo sticks can't breathe on their own.

This would have been inconceivable in the winter, but as it was October, the weather was not cold. And don't forget, Intrepid Reader—the monster known as Twenty Faces loved wild stunts so much that he even considered himself a magician.

Matsuno should have called everyone back at that moment, but he wanted to keep all credit to himself. Instead of asking for help, he attempted to catch the thief on his own. Placing the flashlight on the ground, he reached out and grasped the bamboo and pulled with all his might.

The stick of bamboo was about thirty centimeters long. Sōji had probably been playing with it in the garden and then dropped it somewhere nearby. As Matsuno pulled, the bamboo steadily rose. But bamboo was not all that came up. At the end of the stick was a human hand, smeared black with lake mud. Emerging from the water was a being who looked for all the world like a mud monster, drenched from head to toe.

6   THE FIEND IN THE TREE

AS FOR WHAT HAPPENED on the bank of the lake, Intrepid Reader, I leave it to your imagination.

Six minutes later, Matsuno was once again standing beside the lake, as if nothing had happened. He was breathing a bit heavily, but there was nothing else unusual. He hurried back to the main wing of the house. What could have been the matter? Matsuno seemed to be limping a bit, but he ignored the pain and cut steadily across the garden, arriving at the front gate.

Two houseboys were at this gate, clutching wooden practice swords and keeping strict watch over the premises. Approaching them, Matsuno pressed a hand to his forehead. "I keep getting shivers. I may have a fever. Excuse me while I rest for a bit," he said in a faint voice.

"Ah, it's you, Matsuno. Sure, go take a rest. We'll keep watch for you," one of the houseboys replied, keeping an eye on the garden.

Matsuno thanked them and then disappeared into the garage beside the entrance. Behind it was his room.

Nothing else happened during the night. Not a soul passed through either the front or back gates, and the policemen guarding the outer wall failed to spot anyone suspicious.

At seven the next morning, officers from the Metropolitan Police Department came to inspect the grounds. Everyone inside was forbidden from leaving the estate until they were finished, but they made an exception for the children. Sanae was a senior at the Kadowaki Girls' Academy, and Sōji was in fifth grade at Takachiho Elementary School, so they were escorted out of the manor by the chauffeur as always. Matsuno still seemed a bit under the weather and hardly spoke. But the children could not miss their schooling, so he had to drive.

Chief Inspector Nakamura first interviewed Mr. Hashiba about the study, the scene of the crime. After hearing the details of the case, he sent his men out to inspect the grounds and search the garden.

"No one has left the house since we got home last night, and no one got over the wall, either. You can trust me on this," the man in charge of the local police declared to Nakamura.

"In that case, the thief must still be hiding somewhere inside."

"Exactly. That's the only answer I can think of. But we've been searching since dawn this morning, and have yet to find anything. Nothing but a dog's corpse."

"A, a dog's corpse?"

"To protect themselves against the thief, the family bought a dog named John, but it was poisoned last night. After investigating, we found that at some point Twenty Faces went out into the garden in the guise of the Hashibas' son and fed the dog something. He really was extremely careful. If the little boy hadn't set that trap, he surely would have gotten away with no trouble at all."

"Let's search the garden one more time, then. It's rather large, so there may be a secret hiding place somewhere."

As the two spoke, they suddenly heard a panicked shout from beyond the hill. "Hurry, over here! We found him! We found the thief!"

The voice was accompanied by hurried footfalls from throughout the garden. Guided by the shouts, Chief Inspector Nakamura and the local policeman dashed to the scene. Upon arrival, they realized the voice was that of one of the Hashiba houseboys. He stood under a large beech tree in the grove, pointing up.

"Up there. That man up there has to be the thief! I remember those clothes."

There was a fork in the beech tree about three meters above the base. Hidden by thick leaves, a man lay in the fork in a strange position. Judging by the fact that he was neither making any commotion nor attempting to flee, it appeared that the thief was dead.

Or was he merely unconscious? It was rather ludicrous to think that he had been trying to get some sleep in a situation like this.

"Someone get him down!"

At the chief inspector's orders, a ladder was brought immediately. Four men lifted the thief from the fork and hoisted him down.

"Well, I'll be. He's all tied up!"

Indeed, the villain was bound with thin silk cords. He was also gagged. A handkerchief had been stuffed into his mouth with another tied around it. His clothes were drenched from head to toe, as if he had been caught in a downpour.

Once the gag was removed, the man began to mumble, as if he had suddenly regained consciousness. "Curse him, curse him!"

"Ah, it's Matsuno!" One of the houseboys shouted in surprise.

It was not Twenty Faces. Though he was wearing the thief's clothes, his face was clearly that of Matsuno.

But hadn't Matsuno just left to take Sanae and Sōji to school? What was he doing here?

"What in the world happened to you?" the chief inspector asked.

"Curse that thief! He got me! He got me!" Matsuno screamed in frustration.

7   SŌJI'S WHEREABOUTS

ACCORDING TO MATSUNO'S TESTIMONY, the thief hid and easily escaped from his pursuers. During the chase, Twenty Faces dove into the pond. He had found a hollow tube of bamboo that Sōji had dropped earlier in the garden so he could remain underwater for a long time. He placed one end of the tube in his mouth and stuck the other end up through the surface of the water and quietly breathed as he waited for his pursuers to leave.

But one man stayed behind: the driver, Matsuno, who discovered the bamboo sticking out of the water and figured out the thief's clever trick. After pulling the stick from the water, he came face to face with the muddy fiend.

A fight ensued, but unfortunately Matsuno had no time to call for help. He was pinned down by the thief, who used some silk cords he had in his pocket to bind Matsuno. After changing clothes, Twenty Faces had hoisted Matsuno into the treetop.

The driver who had escorted Sōji and Sanae to school was an impostor! The Hashibas' precious children had been taken who knows where in a car driven by none other than the master thief, Twenty Faces! The shock felt by those involved and the worry filling the hearts of Mr. and Mrs. Hashiba requires no elaboration.

First, they called the Kadowaki Girls' Academy, where Sanae should have been. Surprisingly, they found that she had safely arrived at school. Relieved that the thief apparently did not intend to kidnap their children, they decided to call Sōji's school next—only to find that, although class had already begun, Sōji was nowhere to be found. Mr. and Mrs. Hashiba were aghast.

Twenty Faces may have known that it was Sōji who set the trap. If so, he must have kidnapped the boy in order to get revenge for the wound on his leg.

Naturally, this caused quite an uproar. Chief Inspector Nakamura immediately reported it to the Metropolitan Police Department, which established a cordon around all of Tokyo while searching for the Hashibas' automobile. Luckily, they knew its model and license plate number, so they had all the necessary clues.

Mr. Hashiba called the police station and school nearly every half hour for updates. One, two, and three agonizing hours passed while Sōji's whereabouts remained anyone's guess.

That afternoon, a boy in a slightly soiled coat and a hunting cap appeared at the entrance to the Hashiba estate with an odd message. "'Scuse me. Your driver asked me to come here. He said some kinda personal matter had suddenly come up, so he asked me to bring the car back here. I left it in front of the gate."

The houseboys conveyed this message inside. It was obvious what had happened, so Mr. Hashiba and the steward Kondō rushed to the entrance and inspected the car. It was indeed the Hashiba family's automobile, but there was no one inside. Sōji had been kidnapped after all.

"Look, there's a peculiar envelope sitting here." Kondō picked up an ordinary-looking sealed letter from the cushion. "Confidential Letter for the Eyes of Mr. Hashiba Sōtarō Only" was written in large letters on the front. There was no return address.

"What's this?" Sōtarō wasted no time opening the letter right there at the gate and reading these spine-tingling words:

To: Mr. Hashiba Sōtarō

    Last night, I claimed your diamonds. Now that I have them in my possession they appear more beautiful at every peek. I will treasure them as a family heirloom.

    Aside from my gratitude, I have one small complaint. You see, someone placed a trap in your garden which inflicted a wound on my leg that will take ten days to heal. And as I am entitled to reparations for the injury I suffered, I took your son Sōji with me as a hostage.

    Sōji is currently in the cold basement of my humble abode, sobbing midst the darkness. He was the one responsible for that accursed trap, you see. Wouldn't you agree that a punishment of this sort is only fair?

    Now, about my indemnity: I would like to request the Kannon statue you have in your possession.

    Yesterday, I had the honor of seeing your art room in your home, where I was dazzled by the Kannon's magnificence. There was a card explaining that it was the work of An Ami from the Kamakura period, and it was worthy of being called a national treasure. Naturally, an art lover such as I could not help but lust after it. At that moment, I realized I must find a way to take that statue into my possession, no matter the cost.

    Now then, at exactly ten o'clock tonight, three of my subordinates will appear at your estate, and I would like you to escort them in to the art room. They will take only the Kannon statue and transport it out in a trunk. I will arrange Sōji's return in exchange for the statue. I swear on the name of Twenty Faces that this is no lie.

    You must not inform the police of this. Additionally, you must not follow my subordinates and their trunk. If there is any funny business, Mr. Hashiba, trust that you will never see your son again.

    I believe you will certainly agree to this proposal, but please open the front gate at ten o'clock tonight if you plan to cooperate. I will regard that as the signal to proceed.

    Sincerely,

    Twenty Faces

A more selfish request there never was. Mr. Hashiba clenched his fists in mortification, but with his precious son

Sōji imprisoned by that scoundrel, there seemed to be no choice but to concede to the fiend's audacious orders.

Afterwards, they brought in the young man who had come with the car and questioned him thoroughly. It turned out that he had simply been paid to serve as a messenger and knew not a thing about the thief.

8   THE BOY DETECTIVE

AFTER SENDING THE YOUNG man away Mr. and Mrs. Hashiba sat down in a private room inside, and talked about what to do next with Kondō and Sanae, who had been sent home in a car by the school principal. There was no time to waste, for less than nine hours remained until ten o'clock.

"If it were something else, then I wouldn't mind. All I have to do is part with a little money to replace those diamonds. But that Kannon statue, and *only* that Kannon statue, is something I absolutely cannot part with. Allowing a masterpiece of national treasure quality to fall into the hands of a thief would not benefit the Japanese art world. That sculpture may be locked in our art room, yes, but it's so valuable that I don't even consider it my personal possession."

As expected, Mr. Hashiba wasn't thinking only of his son. The same couldn't be said for Mrs. Hashiba, however; her mind was filled with images of her poor, sweet little boy.

"But if we don't hand over the statue, who knows what will happen to him? No matter how valuable it may be, no piece of art is worth Sōji's life! Please, just do as the thief says, and don't tell the police!"

Vividly unfolding in Mrs. Hashiba's mind was the image of a pitch black basement in an unknown place, with Sōji bawling all alone in the center. She couldn't bear having to wait until ten that night; she wanted to exchange the statue for Sōji without a moment's delay.

"Of course I want him back too, but the very idea of handing that priceless work of art over to that brigand after losing the diamonds to him is so deplorable I can hardly contain myself. Do you have any bright ideas, Kondō?"

"Yes sir, I do have one. If we let the police know, it will make things worse, so I suggest we do our best to keep news of this leaking out until ten o'clock tonight. But, if we were to tell a private detective. . ."

"A private detective, eh? I hadn't thought of that. But could a lone detective take on such a big case?"

"According to what I've heard, sir, there's one very skilled detective living right here in Tokyo."

Watching Kondō with his head cocked, waiting for an answer, Sanae suddenly spoke. "Father, he's talking about Akechi Kogorō! He's so good he even solves cases the police have given up on!"

"Why, yes, Akechi Kogorō. That's the fellow's name. He's truly a brilliant man, so he may be the perfect match for Twenty Faces."

"Yes, I've heard that name before, too. What say we call him right away and have a little discussion then? An expert like him might have an idea."

And so it was decided that Akechi Kogorō would be asked to take on the case.

Without delay, Kondō checked the phone directory and called Akechi Kogorō's home. A boyish voice answered.

"Mr. Akechi is overseas on an important case, and his date of return is not yet set. His assistant Kobayashi is acting as his representative while he is gone. If you have no objection, I can send him over at once."

"Is that so? But this is an extremely difficult case. I'm not sure if an assistant would. . ."

The energetic voice from the other side talked over Kondō. "While 'assistant' may be his official title, Kobayashi is no less skilled than his teacher. You can trust in him, believe me. Anyway, how about I just send him over so you can talk with him?"

"In that case, please ask him if he wouldn't mind coming out here. The villain absolutely must not know of our request, though. This is a life-and-death matter. Please make sure he takes great care not to be seen as he arrives."

"You needn't worry about that. We are professionals here, sir." With that, the master detective known as Kobayashi was sent to the house.

Barely ten minutes after they had hung up, a cute boy appeared at the entrance to the Hashiba estate alone. Upon being shown in and questioned by a houseboy, he introduced himself as a friend of Sōji's.

"The young master isn't home right now."

After hearing this, the boy smiled as if he had known that all along. "I thought that might be the case. Please let me see his father, then. I have a message for him. My name is Kobayashi," he said, concluding the interview.

Hearing the story from his houseboy and recognizing the name Kobayashi, Mr. Hashiba had his visitor led to the parlor. When Mr. Hashiba entered, he saw an apple-cheeked boy of about twelve or thirteen with large eyes.

"Are you Mr. Hashiba? Nice to meet you. I'm Kobayashi, from the Akechi Detective Office. I received a call from you and came at once." The boy opened his eyes wide and spoke very clearly.

"Ah, Mr. Kobayashi's assistant, are you? This is a very complicated matter, son, so I'd rather speak with the man himself."

As Mr. Hashiba talked, the boy lifted his hand to stop him. "No, you see, *I* am Kobayashi Yoshio. There are no other assistants."

"Oh my! *You're* the detective?" Mr. Hashiba asked in shock, feeling strangely amused. *Could this small boy really be a master detective? Judging from his face and the way he speaks, he does seems like a reliable young man. I suppose it wouldn't hurt to chat with him a bit.*

"So the skilled detective they told us about on the phone earlier was you?"

"Yes, that's me. I've been entrusted with all of Mr. Akechi's cases while he's away," Kobayashi said with confidence.

"You said that you were Sōji's friend just a bit ago, didn't you? How do you know Sōji's name?"

"Well, I couldn't expect to do any detective work without knowing at least that much. Your family was featured in a business magazine, so I looked it up and added it to my scrapbook. I was told on the phone that a life was at stake, so I hypothesized that it had to be either Sanae or Sōji who had gone missing. Looks like my hypothesis was correct! And the thief known as Twenty Faces is involved in this case, isn't he?" Kobayashi said with relish.

Maybe this kid really is a genius after all. Mr. Hashiba was thoroughly impressed, so he called in Kondō and explained the details of the case to the boy. Kobayashi listened eagerly, interjecting detailed questions at every critical point. Once the story was finished, he asked to see the Kannon statue. After Mr. Hashiba escorted him to the art room for a look at the object, Kobayashi returned to the waiting room. He closed his eyes and said nothing for a while, seemingly lost in thought.

Finally, the boy's eyes snapped open, and, taking a firm step forward he began speaking energetically. "I've cooked up a clever plan. If he's really a magician, then we'll have to use a little magic ourselves. Now, this will be very dangerous, but nothing is gained without a little danger, right? I've overcome more dangerous situations before."

"Hmm, that sounds promising. Let's hear this plan of yours, then."

"The plan is. . ." Kobayashi suddenly approached Mr. Hashiba and whispered something in his ear.

"Huh? *You* will?" The idea was so outlandish that Mr. Hashiba's eyes nearly popped out of his head.

"That's right. It may seem dangerous at first, but we've already tested it out. Last year in France, Mr. Akechi gave the phantom thief Arsène Lupin a nasty shock using this very method."

"But wouldn't that put Sōji in danger, too?"

"You needn't worry about that. If this were just a petty thief, then it would, but this is Twenty Faces we're talking about, and he would never go back on his word. If he said he'll return Sōji in exchange for the statue, then Sōji will surely be returned before there's any danger. And if by chance Sōji isn't returned, I have another method for escaping that dilemma. Everything will be fine. I may be a child, but I won't do anything rash."

"But it would be terrible if something were to happen to you during Mr. Akechi's absence because we let you do something so dangerous."

Kobayashi chuckled. "Don't you know how we detectives are? Like policemen, we're always prepared to risk everything in the name of duty. This case won't go that far, though. I wouldn't even call this job dangerous. All you have to do is pretend that you haven't seen anything. I have no intention of backing out now, even if you don't assent. I'm ready to act at any moment."

Mr. Hashiba and Kondō didn't know how to respond to the boy's enthusiasm. At the end of the long discussion, it was finally decided that young Kobayashi's plan would be put into action.

9   A Sculpted Miracle

Now let us jump ahead in time to that evening.

At ten o'clock, just as Twenty Faces promised, three rough-looking men passed through the open gate to the Hashiba estate.

The thieves gave sidelong glances to the houseboys stationed at the entrance. "We're here for you-know-what," one remarked in passing. Already knowledgeable about the mansion's floor plan, they marched right into the back without hesitation.

Mr. Hashiba was waiting with Kondō at the entrance to the art room, and called out to one of the criminals. "Now, you haven't broken your promise, I assume. You have my son with you?"

"Don't get yer britches in a bunch," one said brusquely. "The little angel's waitin' at the gate. Ain't no use tryin' to look for him, though. It's all set up so that until we haul out the merchandise, you couldn't find him no matter how hard you searched. Otherwise, we'd be sittin' ducks here."

With that, the trio stomped into the art room. The chamber's earthen walls were lined with glass display cases glowing faintly in the dim light.

Ancient swords, armor, ornaments, cases, folding screens, and hanging scrolls crammed the shelves. In a rectangular glass case in one corner of the room, a meter-and-a-half tall, was the Kannon Statue.

On the lotus seat reposed the dusky Kannon deity, half as large as a man. It had once shined with gilded brilliance, but was now dulled on all sides, and the creases of its many robes were chipped and broken. But it was still clearly a masterpiece, with a perfectly benevolent face that seemed ready to break into a smile at any moment. Any being, no matter how evil, would surely feel compelled to fold their hands and offer a prayer before it.

Even the three thieves seemed to fall under its power, hurrying to finish their work without looking directly at the statue.

"On the double! There ain't no time for dilly-dallyin'!"

As one man spread out a dirty cloth, another grabbed its edges and wrapped it around the glass case. Soon they had covered it so that there was no telling what was inside.

"All right, listen up. If this thing gets turned on its side, it'll break, so be careful!"

Carrying on in a boisterous manner, the three men carried the statue to the front of the house.

Mr. Hashiba and Kondō watched the trio hoist it into the truck. If they let the thieves take the statue without returning Sōji, all would be lost.

Finally, the truck's engine started with a loud roar, and the vehicle was ready to leave.

"Hey, where's Sōji?" Kōndō shouted desperately. "I won't let you leave until you return him! Try and escape, and I'll go straight to the police!"

"I toldja not to worry, didn't I? Turn around. The little pipsqueak's in front of your house!"

Turning around, master and servant saw two shadows at the entrance, one big and one small.

While Mr. Hashiba and Kondō gazed at them, the truck pulled away, receding into the distance. "Toodles!"

The two men dashed to the entrance. "Hey, these are the two beggars who were at our gate earlier. Maybe they were bribed with a free meal." Indeed, it was the father and son that the Hashibas often saw. Both wore tattered old robes and wiped their foreheads with filthy rags.

"What are you two doing? You're not allowed in here!" As Kondō scolded them, the beggars smiled slyly.

"Eheheheheh. But I promised." With this cryptic statement, the tall beggar ran like the wind through the darkness beyond the gate.

"It's me, Father." This next voice belonged to no beggar. The small boy removed a cloth from his face and took off his shabby kimono. Underneath were things that Mr. Hashiba recognized: a school uniform and a pale face.

"Why are you in such filthy clothes?" Mr. Hashiba asked as he embraced his beloved son.

"Who knows? That Twenty Faces scoundrel made me wear them. Until now I was gagged and blindfolded, too."

The tall beggar who just ran off had been none other than Twenty Faces! Disguising himself, he had stood watch to ensure the transfer of the statue was properly completed then returned Sōji as promised before escaping. And what a disguise he had chosen! It wouldn't be unusual to see one or two beggars lurking outside the gates of rich peoples' homes, so it was a perfect choice—and a perfectly fiendish one at that.

Sōji returned home safely. According to the boy, he had been locked in a basement until a little while before, but they had fed him and treated him well. With this, a great weight was lifted from the Hashibas' shoulders. As for how elated Mr. and Mrs. Hashiba were, I'll leave that to your imagination, Intrepid Reader.

After Twenty Faces bolted through the gate in his beggar disguise, he hid in the gloom as he dexterously stripped off the dirty kimono, revealing himself as a brown-robed elderly gentleman. With his white hair and wrinkled skin he looked every bit a retired man in his sixties.

Twenty Faces pulled out a bamboo staff he had hidden on his person and bent his back as he began to shuffle forward. Even if Mr. Hashiba decided to break his promise and give pursuit, Twenty Faces felt confident that his disguise would keep him safe. His thorough preparation was truly admirable.

The old man crossed the street, hailed a taxi, and got in. After directing it in a random direction for twenty minutes, he got out and changed to another, whereupon he rushed to his hideout.

The taxi stopped at the entrance to the Toyamagahara area of Shinjuku, where the old man got out of the taxi and hobbled off. Could this be the location of the phantom's haunt?

At the edge of Toyamagahara's spacious fields, in the middle of a dense cedar wood, sat an old western-style house. It was desolate and appeared to be abandoned. The old man rapped on the door three times, then paused briefly before knocking twice more.

Upon his signal the door swung open. It was one of the thieves who had carried off the statue moments earlier. The old man stepped forward in silence and strode inside. A spacious room that had long since lost its splendor was at the end of the hall. At its center stood the shrouded glass case holding the statue, illuminated by nothing but the ruddy glow of candles.

"Excellent. You three did well. Here's a little reward, so go off and have some fun, would you?"

The trio took the thousand-yen notes he held out and left. Twenty Faces slowly slipped the cloth off the glass box and picked up a nearby candle. Moving directly in front of the statue, he opened the doors to the case.

"O, Kannon, just how skilled a man is Twenty Faces? Two million yen worth of diamonds yesterday and a national treasure today. At this rate, I'll be able to complete my grand art museum in no time at all. Ha ha ha! O, Kannon, what a fine piece of work you are. You almost look alive."

This is the moment you've been waiting for, Intrepid Reader. As Twenty Faces spoke a frightening miracle occurred.

The Kannon statue's wooden right hand shot forward. And in its hand, Intrepid Reader, was not a lotus as there should have been but a pistol aimed directly at the villain's breast!

Now, a sculpture cannot move on its own.

Is that to say, then, that some sort of robotic contraption had been installed inside? Not if it was truly from the Kamakura period. But how else could such a miracle have come about?

Of course, with a pistol aimed right at him, Twenty Faces had no time to ponder such things. He screamed and recoiled, stepping back and putting his hands up even before being told to do so.

10 PITFALL

EVEN THE MASTER THIEF was frightened out of his wits by what he saw. He was not the sort of criminal to be alarmed at the sight of a human opponent, but when this ancient, Kamakura-period Kannon statue suddenly began to move, it was simply too much.

More than surprise, Twenty Faces was filled with a shuddering horror. It was the indescribable fear of a nightmare, or seeing a ghost. Sad as it may seem, the daring, invincible Twenty Faces retreated in pale-faced fright. As if to apologize, he set the candle on the ground and raised both hands high. As he did so, an even more astounding thing happened. Kannon stepped off its lotus pedestal onto the floor and stood erect. Then, keeping its pistol trained on the thief, the statue took three steps forward.

"J-just what a-are you?!" Twenty Faces wailed like a cornered animal.

"Me?" Unbelievable as it seemed, the statue was talking. "I'm the one who's come to take the Hashibas' diamonds back. If you hand them over right now, I'll spare your life," it demanded in a solemn voice.

"Aha! You're a spy from the Hashibas. You disguised yourself as the statue in order to locate my hideout!"

Realizing his opponent was a human being, the thief regained a bit of his spirit, but his fear had not completely evaporated. For one thing, the statue seemed far too short to be a normal person in disguise. Seeing it now, the spy looked to be no taller than an adolescent boy. Listening to this dwarf-like creature calmly order him around was eerie in a way that de-fied explanation.

"And if I refuse to hand over the diamonds?" the thief tim-idly asked his attacker, attempting to distract him.

"Then you will lose your life, plain and simple. This pistol isn't a toy like the ones you always use."

It seemed as if Kannon had already noted this white-haired old man was indeed Twenty Faces in disguise. Perhaps it had heard some of the other thieves talking among themselves earlier.

"Shall I prove it to you?" asked the statue. Its right hand moved with lightning speed, and a shot rang out. One of the windows in the room shattered. The gun had fired a real bul-let! The diminutive Kannon merely glanced at the shards of glass and trained the gun back on his target, his Indian-brown face smirking mischievously. A light blue wisp of smoke waft-ed from the muzzle, which was now pointed at Twenty Faces' heart.

At once, the thief became afraid of just how far this dark-faced little creature might be willing to go. There was no tell-ing what such a reckless, violent person would do next. He might be seriously contemplating murder. And even if Twenty Faces managed to escape the bullets themselves, gunshots would ring out loud and clear to the nearby residents, and who knew what might happen then?

"I have no choice. I'll return the diamonds." He surren-dered, moving to a large desk in a corner of the room. From a hollowed-out leg of the desk he pulled out the six jewels, clink-ing them in his hands as he returned.

"Here they are. Go ahead, inspect them all you want."

The diminutive Kannon extended his left hand. As he took the diamonds, a laugh that one might expect to hear from a shriveled old man escaped his lips.

"Well done, well done. It seems even the great Twenty Faces values his own life."

"Yes, you got me fair and square, I must admit." The thief bit his lip in regret. "By the way, just who are you, anyway? I'm surprised that there was someone else out there clever enough to pull one over on me like this. Would you mind telling me your name?"

"Ha ha ha... How flattering; I'm honored. So you want to know my name? I suppose I should give you something to look forward to once you're behind bars. One of the officers will probably tell it to you eventually." Kannon spoke triumphantly. With his pistol aimed at his foe, he began to retreat to the exit.

He had uncovered the thief's hideout and gotten back the diamonds. Now, all Kannon needed to do was escape this dilapidated shack and seek refuge with the local police. Of course, Intrepid Reader, I am sure you have already puzzled out the true identity of the one behind this disguise: yes, it was none other than Kobayashi Yoshio who turned the tables on the fiendish Twenty Faces for a marvelous victory. And oh, how happy he was! This young lad was such a skilled detective that not even an adult could match him.

But after he had taken a mere three steps out of the room, a queer laughter filled his ears. Turning around, it looked as if the disguised Twenty Faces had been overcome by a fit of hysterics.

That's right, Intrepid Reader. It's far too early to feel relieved. This man was not called a master thief for nothing, you see. Although he made it seem like he had lost, in actuality, Twenty Faces had yet to play his trump card.

"Hey! What's so funny?" The boy who had transformed into a deity cautiously stood with his eyes wide.

Twenty Faces stopped laughing and said "Oh no, I'm sorry. How rude of me. It's just that I've been watching you try so hard to act too big for your britches for so long, I could no longer control myself.

"You see, I've finally figured out who you really are. Not many people can pull the wool over old Twenty Faces' eyes, you know. To be honest, Akechi Kogorō was the first man who came to mind. He isn't such a tiny man, though. You're a child. And as for children who have studied under the Akechi style of detection, there can be only one: Akechi Kogorō's assistant, Kobayashi. . . . Yoshio, was it? Ha ha ha. . . Well? Right on the mark, am I not?"

The boy was stunned at being found out, but realized that since he had already achieved his goal, there was no reason to falter. "Whether that is my name or not, I *am* a child, just as you guessed. If word ever got out that the one and only Twenty Faces himself was foiled by a mere child like me, I imagine it would be quite the reputation breaker." Kobayashi laughed triumphantly.

"Oh, *that's* amusing. You actually think you've defeated the great Twenty Faces, boy?"

"Stop being such a sore loser. The statue you stole came to life, attacked you, and took back the diamonds to boot. You don't call that a loss?"

"That's right. Because I never lose."

"Just what are you planning to do, then?"

"This!"

Kobayashi felt the floorboards go out from under his feet. One moment, his body was floating in empty space. The next, stars filled his eyes and he was wracked by intense pain as he slammed into something with devastating force.

Oh, what a humiliating blunder! You see, Kobayashi had been standing right over a trapdoor and when Twenty Faces pressed a hidden button on the wall, the lock was released, opening into a pitch black hole. Frozen with pain, Kobayashi lay face down in the deep black pit. The gloating guffaws of Twenty Faces echoed from high above.

"Ha ha ha... That must have hurt quite a bit, boy. Poor thing. But for now, I suppose I'll just leave you down there to ponder just how powerful your enemy is. Ha ha ha... Looks like you're still a little bit too young to take on the great Twenty Faces, eh? Ha ha ha!"

11   The Seven Tools

Young Kobayashi lay still in the darkness of the basement for about twenty minutes. His back had taken the brunt of the fall, and the pain was so intense that he couldn't even move.

During those twenty minutes, Twenty Faces mocked the boy, then slammed the trapdoor shut. There was no hope—he was a prisoner. If the thief decided not to feed him, Kobayashi would die alone in this decrepit basement without anyone ever finding out.

How could anyone expect a boy of his age to cope with such frightening circumstances? Most boys would break down and sob when faced with such loneliness, fright, and despair. But young Kobayashi neither cried nor despaired. Courageously, he still refused to believe that he had truly lost to Twenty Faces. Once the pain in his back had eased, he lifted off the torn cloth he had disguised himself with and touched a small canvas satchel hanging from his shoulder.

"Pippo, are you all right?" As he asked the strange question, he stroked the bag from the outside. Something tiny inside shifted. "Looks like you didn't get hit anywhere, did you, Pippo? As long as you're here, I won't feel the least bit lonely."

Confirming that nothing unfortunate had happened to Pippo, Kobayashi sat down in the darkness and removed the small satchel. He pulled out a pen flashlight, which he used to illuminate the floor and pick up the six diamonds and the pistol. Putting them in the satchel, he then inspected its contents thoroughly to make sure nothing had been lost.

Sure enough, the boy's seven detective tools were all still there. The legendary monk warrior Musashibō Benkei, who served the hero Yoshitsune in the Heian period, is said to have carried a variety of tools on his back for use in battle, popularly known as Benkei's Seven Tools. Kobayashi's seven detective tools were by no means large weapons. In fact, they were small enough that all seven would fit in his hands. But in terms of usefulness, they could hold their own against those of Benkei's.

First was the pen flashlight. During night investigations, there is nothing more important to a detective than possessing a light source, especially one like this that could also serve as a signal.

Next came the pocket utility knife. With a saw blade, scissors, awl and more, it was an all-purpose tool ready for any situation.

Then there was the rope ladder made from sturdy silk cord, compact enough to fit in the palm of one's hand when wrapped. A pen-sized telescope, watch, compass, and small notebook with a pencil accounted for the remaining tools, supplemented this time with the pistol Kobayashi had used to threaten Twenty Faces.

And last but not least, we mustn't forget little Pippo. As Kobayashi shined his flashlight through the satchel, he finally came upon a lone pigeon. The cute little bird huddled patiently in a separate pocket.

"Pippo, I know it's a bit tight in there, but just hang on for a little bit longer. If you get caught by that monster, you'll be in big trouble." Kobayashi stroked the bird's head. The bird cooed in reply, as if it had understood what he said. Pippo was the boy detective's pet, and as long as they were together, Kobayashi had faith that they could escape any danger.

But that wasn't all. Aside from emotional support, this pigeon had another important mission: it was a messenger, for communications are of the utmost importance to detectives at work. Policemen have radios in their cars for precisely this reason, but unfortunately private detectives don't have access to such luxuries. Hiding a pocket transceiver under one's clothing would be best, but it wasn't the type of item a boy could easily obtain. Kobayashi had come up with the clever idea of using a carrier pigeon instead.

It was a childish idea—but the imagination of children can sometimes bring forth results that surprise even adults. "Inside this satchel, I have both a radio and an airplane," Kobayashi proudly announced. Indeed, this carrier pigeon functioned as both.

After checking on his seven tools, the boy put his satchel back under the cloth with satisfaction and then began to investigate the basement with his flashlight. The room was roughly fourteen square meters in area, with concrete walls on all four sides. It looked to have been used as a storage room in the past. Thinking there had to be a stairway somewhere, Kobayashi looked around and found there was a large wooden ladder hung on the ceiling. Simply sealing the exits hadn't been enough—in an extremely cautious move, Twenty Faces had gone as far as to remove the stairs altogether. At this rate, who knew if escape was actually possible?

Aside from a sofa with one broken leg and an old blanket thrown over it in the corner, there was no other object visible in the room. It felt like a prison cell.

As he stared at the sofa, something crossed Kobayashi's mind. "Hashiba Sōji was kept here, too, and he must have slept on that sofa." Feeling a bit sentimental as he pondered this, Kobayashi approached the sofa. He tested the cushions and then pulled out a hideaway bed.

"Guess I'll try and get a little shuteye," he muttered, and plopped down on the bed. Kobayashi had to save his courage until dawn—that's when he would act. It made perfect sense, but most boys wouldn't be able to calmly take a nap in such a situation!

"C'mon, Pippo, let's get some rest. Hopefully we'll have a good dream or two." Kobayashi clutched the precious satchel to his breast and closed his eyes to the dark.

Soon, the tranquil sounds of a boy sleeping soundly drifted from the sofa bed.

12   THE CARRIER PIGEON

WHEN KOBAYASHI AWOKE, HE was astonished to find he was not in the bedroom of the detective office as usual and suddenly recalled what had happened.

"Oh, right, I'm locked in this basement. It's pretty bright for a basement, though."

The dreary walls and floor were dimly lit, despite the fact that no sunlight should have been able to reach this underground chamber. Kobayashi looked around and spotted a small skylight in the ceiling. He hadn't noticed it the night before.

It was small—only thirty centimeters on a side—and with thick iron bars attached. The window was about three meters from the floor but was most likely at ground level seen from the outside.

"Let's see if we can't sneak out through that window," thought Kobayashi, jumping off the sofa and running under the window to look up at the bright sky. There was a pane of glass in the window, but it was broken, so a passerby might hear him if he shouted loudly.

Kobayashi pushed the sofa under the window and tried using it as a step stool, but he was still out of reach.

Is this to say that despite Kobayashi's detection of the window, he wouldn't even be able to look through it? Now, now, Intrepid Reader, no need to waste your concern on such a trifling obstacle. After all, it was precisely for moments like these that Kobayashi carried with him the rope ladder. In short, he'd already found a use for another of the seven tools. Kobayashi pulled it from his satchel and stretched it out. Holding it with slack like a cowboy with a lasso, he aimed the hook on one end at the window's bars.

After missing a few times, he finally heard a clink from the other end: the hook had caught firmly on one of the bars.

The rope ladder itself was a fairly simple construction, stretching a total of five meters. It was a long, sturdy silk cord with knots every twenty centimeters for climbing. Kobayashi was not as strong as an adult, but when it came to apparatus gymnastics, he was second to none. The young detective climbed the rope with ease and managed to grab on to the steel bars.

Upon closer inspection, though, he sadly realized that the bars were embedded deeply in concrete. It would take much more than a mere utility knife to cut them out.

But what about shouting in a loud voice from the hole? Unfortunately, there seemed to be no potential in that option, either. The window opened onto an overgrown garden thick with grass and trees, beyond which lay a hedge and a wide field with no road to be seen. He could simply wait for some children to come and play in the field and then attempt to seek help, but it was doubtful his voice would carry that far.

And worse, if he did scream loud enough for people in the field to hear him, the one person his voice would undoubtedly reach first was, of course, Twenty Faces. *No way, that's out of the question. I can't possibly take such a risk.*

Young Kobayashi had reached an impasse, but in spite of his situation he made a valuable discovery. Until this very moment, he hadn't had any idea exactly where this building was, but the view through the window had given him all the clues he needed.

Yes, Intrepid Reader, I hear you loud and clear. No one could figure out where they were just by looking out a window. But Kobayashi did—through a perfect stroke of luck! Outside the window, far beyond the wide field, he could see some buildings unlike any others in Tokyo. Readers from Tokyo will of course be familiar with the big concrete buildings lining the streets of Toyamagahara like featureless white blocks. Wouldn't you agree, Intrepid Reader, that this nondescript quality would be an ideal landmark?

The young detective input the location of the thief's house in relation to the buildings into his brain and then climbed down the rope ladder. Hurriedly opening his satchel, he took out his notebook and compass, verified his orientation, and sketched out some maps. It was clear that his prison was in the west corner of the north side of Toyamagahara. Once again, the seven tools had served him well!

Looking at his watch, Kobayashi saw it was just past six in the morning. The room upstairs was dead quiet, so perhaps Twenty Faces was still fast asleep.

"Ah, I can't believe this! I've gotten myself to Twenty Faces' secret hideout and now know exactly where it is, but I still can't arrest him!" Kobayashi shouted in frustration, curling his hands into fists.

If only I could shrink in size and grow wings like a fairy from a storybook. Then I could go straight to the police station, guide the officers here, and catch Twenty Faces once and for all! The boy sighed as he continued to daydream. While fantasizing in this way, suddenly a wonderful idea occurred to him. *Oh boy, am I stupid! Of course I can do that! I have my airplane Pippo right here with me!* His face flushed with happiness, and his heart began beating faster.

Hands shaking with excitement, Kobayashi marked down the location of the thief's lair in his notebook along with the information about his entrapment then ripped out the page and folded it neatly. Taking the carrier pigeon out of his satchel, Kobayashi stuck his letter into a small tube tied to the bird's legs and tightly sealed it.

"Okay, Pippo, it's time for you to save the day. You gotta bolt straight back there. No stopping for a snack along the way.

Got it? Now fly through that window and hurry on back to Mr. Akechi's!"

Pippo sat in the palm of Kobayashi's hand and listened to every word, flitting its cute eyes to and fro. Once Pippo looked like it understood its mission, the pigeon spread its wings gallantly, flew around the basement a couple of times, then shot out the window.

Ah, good. In about ten minutes, Pippo should be back to Mr. Akechi's wife at home. She'll call the police at once. That's for sure. It'll probably be about thirty minutes until they get here! Maybe forty! Either way, we should have the thief caught within the hour, and then I'll finally be able to get out of this hole.

Staring at the sky that Pippo had disappeared into, Kobayashi became lost in thought. He became so lost in thought, in fact, that he didn't notice one bit as the doors to the pitfall were opened.

"And just what might you be doing over there, little Kobayashi?" The familiar voice of Twenty Faces struck the boy's ears like thunder.

Kobayashi widened his eyes as he turned to look up. Peeking upside down through the square trapdoor was the white-haired head of the thief, looking just as he had appeared the night before. Oh no! Did this mean he saw Pippo go flying off too? Kobayashi stared straight into the fiend's eyes, his hopeful smile suddenly draining away.

13 A Curious Negotiation

"So, how did you sleep last night, Mr. Boy Detective? Ha ha ha. What's that hanging from the window there, a black rope? Hah! So you had a rope ladder prepared, did you? Excellent work! Bravo! You really are a clever boy. Although I doubt you can remove the steel bars on that window with your own strength alone. And you know what? Standing there crying and glaring at that window won't help you to escape one bit. A real shame, ain't it?" the fiend taunted.

"Oh, good morning. Actually, I wasn't planning on escaping at all. In fact, it's so nice and comfy down here that I've even taken a liking to this room. I think I'm going to stay for a while." Kobayashi hadn't been defeated in the slightest. He had been a little worried that the thief might have seen the carrier pigeon flying out through the window, but judging from the way the man spoke now that clearly wasn't the case. He no longer felt the slightest bit of anxiety.

As long as Pippo made it safely to the detective office, everything would be all right. No matter what cruel words Twenty Faces might hurl at him, they couldn't hurt Kobayashi at all. He knew he'd have the last laugh.

"Comfy, eh? Bravo all the more! I would expect no less from Akechi's right-hand man. But Kobayashi, isn't there one thing you're worried about? I imagine you're quite hungry by now, hmm? Or are you planning on starving to death as well?"

Clearly, Twenty Faces had no idea that the police were probably on their way to his house at that very moment, having received Pippo's report. Kobayashi said nothing, silently laughing to himself.

"Ha ha ha. Looks like that disheartened you a bit. Allow me to bring you some good news, then. You're going to pay an expensive fee, and in exchange I'll let you have a delicious, mouthwatering breakfast! No, no, I'm not talking about money. In exchange for food, I want that pistol you brought here. If you quietly hand it over to me like a good little boy, then I'll order my cook to bring you breakfast at once. How does that sound?" Twenty Faces was obviously unsettled by the existence of the pistol, and with good reason. Requesting it in exchange for breakfast was a clever idea.

Believing he would eventually be saved, Kobayashi had little difficulty bearing his hunger for a bit longer. Showing the thief too smug a face, however, would only arouse suspicion. And besides, at this point he no longer had any use for the pistol.

"It's unfortunate, but I suppose I'll have to agree to this deal of yours. To be honest, I'm starving," he answered with feigned regret.

Not recognizing this as an act, but assuming his plans had gone perfectly, the villain smirked with conceit. "Heh heh heh. I thought as much, my boy. Looks like you can't win against your appetite, can you? As you wish. I'll bring out the food right away." Twenty Faces closed the trapdoor once he had finished speaking, but the sound of him ordering the cook to prepare breakfast could be faintly heard through the floor.

Preparing the food took a surprisingly long time, and by the time Twenty Faces opened the trapdoor and showed his face again, twenty minutes had passed.

"Here we are, little Kobayashi, a hot breakfast with your name on it. I expect the fee beforehand, mind you. So go on and place the pistol in this basket."

A small basket attached to a rope came sliding smoothly down. Obeying the fiend's orders, Kobayashi placed the pistol inside, and the basket was quickly reeled back up. The second time it dropped down, it contained three steaming rice balls, some ham, a raw egg, and a bottle of tea. For a prisoner, it was quite a feast.

"That's right, take your time. You paid your fee, so I'll give you as long as you want. But for lunch, I'll be expecting the diamonds, boy. I know it may be hard to part with them after all your hard work, but I intend to reclaim those jewels one by one. And remember, no matter how painful it may seem, you've got your hunger to worry about. In other words, those diamonds are still, and have always been, as good as mine! One by one, one by one. . . Ha ha ha. I'm so glad you decided to check in to my little hotel!"

To Twenty Faces, this curious negotiation of his was just too amusing to keep quiet about. But with such a patient method, would he really be able to reclaim all the diamonds? Or, before any of that could even happen, would *he* become the prisoner instead?

14   KOBAYASHI'S VICTORY

As HE PERCHED OVER the trapdoor bouncing the freshly taken pistol in his hands, Twenty Faces felt on top of the world. Just as he opened his mouth to torment Kobayashi even further, a sound rang out.

The pitter-patter of footsteps running down from the second floor was followed by the appearance of the cook's frightened face. "We got trouble, sir. Three cars filled with cops stormed the house, and from where I saw 'em through the second floor window, it looks like they're just outside the gate. We gotta book it!"

Yes, Pippo had completed his mission just as he was supposed to, and the police had arrived even earlier than Kobayashi had expected. Listening to the commotion above, the boy detective felt happy enough to leap right out of the pit.

Even Twenty Faces couldn't help but feel flabbergasted by the surprise attack. "What?" he moaned, jumping up and dashing to the front entrance, forgetting to close the trapdoor. By the time he got to the door, it was already too late. The sounds of pounding could be heard from the other side. Putting his eye to the peephole next to the door, the thief saw a sea of uniformed policemen.

"Curses!" This time Twenty Faces headed to the rear door, his body quaking with anger, but before he could get there, it too, began to echo with a violent pounding. In a flash, his lair had been completely surrounded!

"We're done for, boss! There ain't no way outta here!" the cook shouted in despair.

"Our only hope is the second floor, then." Twenty Faces meant they were going to hide in the attic.

"That won't work. They'll sniff us out right away!" The cook was screaming so loud it almost seemed like he was going to cry. Ignoring him, the master thief took the man's hand and dragged him to the attic stairs.

Just after the two disappeared, a thundering noise crackled out from the front door. Before it even hit the floor, a crowd of policemen surged through, rushing into the house. At almost exactly the same time, the back door also burst open, and more officers poured in.

The man in charge was once again Chief Inspector Nakamura, the "Demon of the Department." He positioned high-ranking officers at the front and back doors, then ordered the remaining men to search every nook and cranny of every room.

"Ah, here it is. The basement!" one policeman barked from atop the trapdoor. Other officers soon flocked around it. A man bent down to peek into the dim cement pit, where he saw Kobayashi.

"There he is! So you're Kobayashi!" he called out.

The boy had been waiting. "That's right. Hurry and lower the ladder please!"

Meanwhile, the rooms on the first floor had all been searched top to bottom, but the thief was nowhere to be found.

"Kobayashi, do you know where Twenty Faces went?" Finally lifting the strangely dressed boy out of the basement, Nakamura hurriedly questioned him.

"He was right here just a moment ago. He can't have escaped outside. The second floor, maybe?"

Just as Kobayashi finished his last syllable, a blood-curdling scream sounded from the second floor.

"Hurry, everyone! It's Twenty Faces! We got him!"

Policemen came charging in response, stampeding up the stairway at the back of the corridor. Loud footsteps stormed

up to the attic, where there was only a single tiny window, making it as dark as night.

"Here, right here! Hurry! Give me a hand!"

In the faint light, a single policeman could be seen shouting as he pinned down a white-haired, white-bearded man. The old man seemed quite powerful, as if he had only been tackled after considerable effort and could strike back at any moment.

A few men ran ahead at first to help keep the old man pinned down. Following them, four, five, and then six men all swooped down on the thief, piling on top of one another. No matter how fearsome Twenty Faces claimed to be, resistance was no longer an option, and his arms and legs were quickly and securely bound. Finally, when the white-haired old man was completely tired out and cowering in the corner, Nakamura brought in Kobayashi. They had to be sure.

"This is Twenty Faces, correct?"

The boy nodded immediately. "Yes. That's him. Twenty Faces was disguised just like this!"

"Put him in the car, men. And make sure he doesn't try to pull a fast one on you!" the chief ordered. Officers stood the thief up, surrounded him on all four sides, and frog-marched him downstairs.

"Kobayashi, my boy, you did an excellent job. I'm sure Mr. Akechi will be quite surprised when he returns from overseas. This is *the* Twenty Faces you caught, after all. Tomorrow, your name will echo through all the nation."

Nakamura took the boy detective's hands, clutching them with eternal gratitude.

Thus, the battle ended in Kobayashi's victory. The Hashibas still had their statue, and all six diamonds were now safe in the boy's satchel. It was a complete victory, without any shortcomings. After all his hard work, the criminal had not only failed to acquire any of the items he wished, but had also lost his prisoner Kobayashi, and then finally got arrested himself.

"For some reason, it almost seems too easy. I can't believe I've actually beaten Twenty Faces," Kobayashi said in disbelief, his face pale from excitement.

Overcome with joy from arresting the thief, Kobayashi had completely forgotten one small matter: the whereabouts of Twenty Faces' cook. Just where had *he* disappeared to? Is it not strange that throughout the police's extensive searches the man had never shown himself?

He certainly hadn't had time to escape. After all, if the cook was able to escape, then Twenty Faces would have escaped as well. Was he still hiding somewhere in the house, then? That too would be impossible. It's unthinkable that a blunder of such magnitude had occurred during the officers' thorough inspection.

Intrepid Reader, I invite you to place this book down for a moment and think. Just what is the true meaning behind our cook's bizarre vanishing act?

15 A Terrifying Challenge

Two hours after the arrest at the abandoned house in Toyamagahara, the Fiend with Twenty Faces was interrogated in a gloomy chamber of the Metropolitan Police Department. Inside, Chief Inspector Nakamura and the disguised thief faced each other across a single desk. The criminal stood arrogantly, arms still tied behind his back. He had yet to utter a single word.

"You mind showing us your real face for a moment?"

The chief approached Twenty Faces' side, suddenly grabbing the white hair and ripping off the wig. From underneath, a dirty head was visible. Next, he plucked off the full-face beard, revealing the villain's true face.

"Wow, that's one ugly mug you've got there!"

The chief's face contorted with horror as he spoke, and it was well-warranted. The thief had a narrow brow, frizzy uneven eyebrows, and glowing bug eyes beneath them. Together with his flat nose and thick lips, there wasn't a single appealing feature about him. He looked truly unrefined, like a wild man from the jungle.

As described earlier, Twenty Faces possessed a number of utterly different faces. He was a monster who could transform himself into old men, young men, and even women at times, which meant that not only the public but the entire police force had absolutely no idea what he actually looked like. And yet, what a grisly face he possessed! It was possible that this monstrous visage was only another of the man's disguises.

Chief Nakamura got an eerie feeling unlike anything he'd ever experienced before. Glaring at the criminal's face, he couldn't help but raise his voice.

"Tell me now: is that honestly your real face?!" Indeed, it was a strange question. But the chief truly believed that this strange question was one he had to ask. The thief remained silent, letting his big lips spread open in a wide smirk.

Seeing that, Nakamura felt a shiver run down his spine, and he began to feel that something stranger than he could possibly imagine was happening before his very eyes. To hide his fear, the chief moved even closer, raising both hands and pulling on the thief's face. He tried pulling off the man's eyebrows, tried pushing on his nose, tried twisting his cheeks, as if he were playing with a toy. But no matter what he tried, it only became more apparent that the man was not disguised. As unlikely as it seemed, the villain who had once disguised himself as the handsome Hashiba Sōichi possessed the face of an ogre.

"Heh heh. C'mon, that tickles! Cut it out already, would ya?" The thief finally spoke—and with such an uncultured voice! There wasn't a scrap of grace in the way he talked, and it sounded like he was mocking the police. Or perhaps. . .

The chief widened his eyes and glared at the arrested man once more. A single outrageous thought dawned on him. But wait, could such a feat actually be possible? It seemed too preposterous a fantasy. No, it was absolutely impossible. But the chief had to make sure.

Then came another unthinkable question. "Who are you? Just who are you?"

But this question the criminal heeded, as if he had been anticipating it. "The name's Kinoshita Torakichi. I'm a cook."

"Shut up! You're just making that stupid voice on purpose and trying to trick me. I'm on to you, buster! Now tell me the truth. Twenty Faces is an infamous master thief! He wouldn't try something so cowardly!"

After getting screamed at so much, one would expect the man to at least flinch. And what did this thief do but suddenly break out into a hearty laugh!

"Woowee! Little old me, Twenty Faces? That's a good one! You think Twenty Faces is a dirty old fool like me? Guess you've got no eyes for thieves, officer. C'mon, how much more obvious could this be?"

Nakamura lost his composure completely. "Shut up! I don't want to hear any more of your lies. This is ludicrous! Kobayashi identified you as Twenty Faces right at the scene!"

"Wa ha ha. Yeah, well the kid sure struck out on that one! I don't remember committing any crimes, either, y'know. I'm just a little old cook. Twenty Faces, Ten Faces, call me whatever you want. But I ain't none other than the lowly ol' cook Torakichi who he hired at that house ten days ago. Go ahead, ask my supervisor. You'll find it all checks out."

"And why would a perfectly innocent cook be disguised as an old man like that?"

"Well, that's simply because I was suddenly tackled, then forced to put these clothes on and wear this wig. To be honest, I really don't have any idea what's going on either, officer. The minute you and your boys came a-knockin', the boss just grabbed my hand and dragged me upstairs.

"There's a hidden wardrobe in that room with a bunch of disguises and costumes in it. The boss pulled a police uniform and cap out from there, hurried and put it on, then put the old man costume he had been wearing on me. Then all of a sudden he started shouting, 'It's Twenty Faces!' and pinned me down so I couldn't move. Thinking back on it now, officer, I guess he was acting like he was one of your men who had just caught Twenty Faces—or himself, I guess. That attic's mighty dim, and in the middle of all that ruckus, you can't really be sure of people's faces, see? There was nothing I could do. The boss is as strong as a horse, y'know."

With his face pale and stiff, Nakamura silently pressed the bell on the table over and over. An office boy popped his head in, and the chief ordered that the four officers entrusted with watching over the front and rear exits to the Toyamagahara house that morning be sent in at once.

Soon, the four entered the room only to be met with a chilling gaze from their superior. "When you arrested this man, no one left the house, correct? He may have been wearing one of our uniforms. Did you see anyone?"

"One officer did go out," one policeman answered. "He shouted that the thief had been caught and to go to the second floor, then ran downstairs and outside as we all charged up."

"Why didn't you say anything about this until now? You didn't get a good look at his face, did you? Even if he was wearing a uniform, you could have easily determined whether he was an impostor or not by looking at him!" An engorged vein pulsed lividly on the chief's forehead.

"But we didn't have time to look at his face! He ran like the wind and jumped out in a flash. I did think it was suspicious, though, so I asked him where he was going. As he ran, he said that you had ordered him to use the phone, sir. That's the standard procedure we've done numerous times before, so I didn't think anything of it. Besides, the thief had already been caught, so I forgot all about him, and didn't report it."

The policeman's story certainly sounded reasonable. So reasonable, in fact, that it only added shock value to how smoothly and carefully the thief had carried out his plan.

There was no longer any doubt. The barbaric, ogre-faced man before them was far from a master thief: he was an insignificant cook and nothing more. Just thinking about the dozens of policemen who had created that huge ruckus to capture this useless pawn left the chief and his four subordinates staring blankly at each other in stupefaction.

"Anyways, officer, the boss wrote something that he told me to give you." Torakichi pulled a crumpled piece of paper from his robe and handed it to the chief.

Nakamura snatched it from the man, smoothed it out and quickly inspected it, his face turning purple with rage.

Written on the paper was the following absurdity:

> To: Nakamura Zenshirō:
>
> Be sure and give my regards to Kobayashi. He is truly a fine young boy. Oh yes, he's absolutely adorable. But no matter how cute little Kobayashi may be, I cannot sacrifice my freedom for him. It's too bad for the child, as I expect he's drunk with victory right now, but I thought I'd teach him a little about how the real world works. Tell him that he should stop trying to resist Twenty Faces with that tiny little child brain of his and that if he doesn't stop now, he's going to end up biting off far more than he can chew.
>
> And, officers of the law, allow me to let slip a bit of my future plans. The situation with the Hashibas ended unfortunately, but I won't torment them any further. I've just about had it with that meager art room of theirs, and at this very moment, I'm quite busy preparing for a much bigger caper. I imagine that news of this grand affair will be reaching your ears in the near future— in which case, I look forward to meeting you again.
>
> Twenty Faces

Intrepid Reader, I regret to inform you that in the end, the battle between Twenty Faces and the young Kobayashi concluded with the master thief's victory. Twenty Faces sneered at the Hashibas' vault and boasted that he was already planning to steal something even greater. Just what could this grand plan be? It was quite possible that a boy such as Kobayashi would not be able to stand up to him this time around. Everyone was awaiting the return of Akechi Kogorō. After all, it couldn't be that much longer!

Ah, the showdown between master detective Akechi Kogorō and the Fiend with Twenty Faces—a one-on-one battle of wits! Just how much longer will this excruciating wait continue?

16   THE ART FORTRESS

FORTY KILOMETERS SOUTH FROM the Shūzenji Hot Springs on the Izu Peninsula, tucked deep in the mountains off the Shimoda Highway, is a rather lonely community called Taniguchi Village. Nestled within the forest beyond the village stood an austere manor that looked strangely like a castle.

It was surrounded by a tall earthen wall capped with a long line of sharp metal spikes, standing like the spines of a cactus. Inside the wall, a four-meter-wide moat filled with bright green water surrounded the building. Clearly designed to keep people away, the moat was deeper than a grown man. Even if someone managed to climb over the spiked wall, they would only fall into a deep green trap. There were no watchtowers in the compound, but massive, thick-walled, white storehouses with tiny windows loomed in the vicinity.

The locals called the place "Kusakabe's Castle," but that was no more than a colorful nickname. A castle would never have been built for such a small settlement. Who lived behind those well-fortified walls, then? If this were the un-policed Warring States period it wouldn't have been anything out of the ordinary. But not even the richest of the rich these days would build such an extravagant lair.

"Who in the world lives there?"

Every time a traveler asked this question, the villagers answered exactly the same way. "In there? That's crazy old Mr. Kusakabe's Castle. He's an eccentric so afraid of having his treasures stolen that he doesn't even talk to his own neighbors!"

The Kusakabe family had owned land in this area for generations, until the current heir, Samon, sold off almost everything. All that remained was the citadel itself, filled to the brim with priceless ancient masterpieces.

Samon, now an old man, was a crazed art collector. Most of his collection consisted of classic pieces, such as paintings by Sesshu and Tanyū. He was so obsessed with amassing art that it would be safe to say he had collected works by just about every classical artist famous enough to be featured in an elementary school textbook. The hundreds of scrolls there included masterpieces on the order of national treasures, rumored to be worth billions of yen.

Now you should understand why Kusakabe's Castle was so fortified: Samon valued these pieces more than his life. Day and night, awake or asleep, he did nothing but worry about them being stolen.

He dug a moat and installed spikes on top of the wall but still had no peace of mind. It got to the point where he would stare suspiciously into the eyes of any visitor, certain they were just another thief attempting to rob him, so he no longer communicated with any of the honest villagers.

Thus, Samon hid in his castle all year round, surrounded by his beloved collection. He hardly ever went outside, and his art mania was so severe that he had never longed for a wife, leaving him childless. Before he knew it, Samon was over sixty and had lived his entire adult life as if he had been born to watch over art. This, Intrepid Reader, was the eccentric master of the curious Art Fortress.

One day Samon was sitting deep in one of the white-walled storehouses as usual, basking in the glow of his ancient masterpieces as if he were in heaven.

Outside the sun shone gently, but the tiny, barred windows of Samon's complex kept the room as cold and dark as a prison.

"Master, please open up. You've received a letter," came the voice of an elderly butler from outside. The only servants Samon kept in his spacious estate were this old man and his wife.

"A letter? How unusual. Bring it here." As he answered, the old wooden door creaked open, and an elderly man just as wrinkled as his master entered with a single letter in his hand.

Samon took the document and looked on the back for the sender's name, but strangely enough it was blank. "Who could it be from? I wasn't expecting anything like this."

But it was clearly addressed to Mr. Kusakabe Samon, so he cut open the envelope and began to read.

"Good heavens, sir, what's the problem? Is it something terrible?" shouted the butler, alarmed by the dramatic change in Samon's expression. His beardless, creased face sagged, the lips of his toothless mouth began to quiver, and the eyes behind his spectacles flashed with fear.

"No, it's n-nothing. Nothing you would understand. Now leave me be." Samon managed to shoo his butler out with a quivering voice, but this letter was by no means "nothing." It was so far from "nothing," in fact, that it was a wonder the old man didn't faint on the spot.

In the letter, these chilling words were written:

To: Mr. Kusakabe Samon

> Forgive this sudden communication, but I'm sure the newspapers can adequately introduce my humble self. To explain matters simply, I have decided to claim every last one of the ancient art pieces in your collection, leaving not a scroll behind. I will come on the night of November 15.
>
> Barging in all of a sudden and surprising an elderly gentleman like you would be far too cruel, so I will announce the exact time at a later date.

Twenty Faces

Ah, so the Fiend with Twenty Faces had finally set his sights on the mad art collector of mountainous Izu! About a month had passed since he had disguised himself as a policeman and fled his hideout at Toyamagahara. During that time, no one had any idea where Twenty Faces was or what he was doing. He had most likely found a new hiding place, hired new henchmen, and was working hard at his next evil plan. And now, out of all the possible candidates for his next crime, he had selected the surprisingly rustic locale of Kusakabe's Art Fortress.

November 15? But that's tonight! Ah, what should I do? Now that Twenty Faces has set his sights on me, I might as well kiss my precious treasures goodbye. Not even the Metropolitan Police Department could do anything about that monstrous thief! The hapless police out here in the country won't even be able to touch him.

Ah, this is the end for me! I'd rather die than watch all my treasures get taken away!

Samon suddenly stood, unable to keep still, and began pacing around the room.

I'm completely out of luck. There's no way to avoid this now! Before he knew it, his wrinkled face was wet with tears. *Wait, wait a moment. Ah yes, I remember. I remember now! Why did it take me so long? Oh, God, you haven't yet forsaken me, have you? If I can only get that man here, then I might be saved!*

Recalling something, Samon's face suddenly brimmed with vitality.

"Hey, Sakuzō! Sakuzō, are you there?" He stepped outside and called for his butler, clapping his hands loudly. The old butler came running at the sound of his master's frantic voice.

"Bring me a copy of the *Izu Daily*. I'm pretty sure it was yesterday's edition, but it doesn't matter. Just bring three or four days' worth here. Go on, hurry. Hurry!" he ordered harshly.

In a flurry, Sakuzō hurried off and brought back copies of the local newspaper. Samon impatiently flipped through each page of the local news section. Just as he remembered, the following was written in the news section on the thirteenth:

The Art Fortress

AKECHI KOGORŌ'S HOMECOMING

Japan's leading private detective, Mr. Akechi Kogorō, has finally completed his missions abroad and returned home to Tokyo. However, in order to recover from his fatigue, he is leaving again today on a week-long trip to the Fujiya Inn at Shūzenji Hot Springs.

"This is it, this is it! This detective Akechi is the only man capable of taking on Twenty Faces! Just think of the great work his assistant Kobayashi did during the Hashiba incident, and he was a mere child! Detective Akechi will surely be able to save me tonight. I'm going to have to get him over here, no matter what!"

Mumbling this, Samon had Sakuzō call his wife, who helped the old man put on his kimono. He locked the sturdy wooden doors to his treasure rooms from the outside and ordered his two servants to keep watch while he left the estate.

Of course, Samon was headed straight to the nearby Fujiya Inn. He hoped to meet with detective Akechi and ask him to protect his treasures.

Yes, Intrepid Reader, that's right—the long-awaited Akechi Kogorō had finally returned! Not only that, but he was in the right place at the right time, enjoying the hot springs right next to Kusakabe's Castle, the very place Twenty Faces was scheduled to attack that night. It was as if everything had been prepared perfectly, and it filled Samon with more hope than ever.

17 MASTER DETECTIVE AKECHI KOGORŌ

WRAPPED IN A MOUSE-COLORED Inverness coat, the small-statured Samon scurried down a long hill. He reached the Fujiya Inn around one in the afternoon.

"Where is Mr. Akechi Kogorō?" he asked, only to learn that the detective had gone fishing behind the inn. Asking a maid to show him the way, Samon strode briskly to the mountain stream.

Following a dangerous path thick with bamboo grass, the deep valley opened to a stream where the beautiful sound of babbling water could be heard. Beyond large steppingstones, a lone man in a padded kimono sat on the biggest flat rock, bent over and peering intently at his drooping fishing rod.

"That's Mr. Akechi." The maid hopped deftly over the rocks toward the detective. "Excuse me, sir, there's a man here who has come to meet with you."

Annoyed, Akechi turned to face her. "Don't speak so loudly. The fish will scatter," he scolded.

Disheveled, unkempt hair, sharp eyes, and slightly pallid skin. A high nose, clean shaven face, and straight, powerful lips. Without a doubt this was the detective Akechi Kogorō who Samon had seen in photographs.

"I am Kusakabe Samon," said the treasure collector, extending his calling card. "I have come here with a request for you, sir." He bowed slightly.

Detective Akechi accepted the calling card, but didn't really look at it. "Oh, really? And what kind of request would that be?" he said in an impatient tone, focusing more on his fishing rod.

Samon ordered the maid to go back, watching her until she left. "The truth is, detective, I received this letter today."

Removing Twenty Faces' announcement from his pocket, Samon thrust it in front of the detective, who was still paying more attention to the fish.

"Ah, that little guy got away again. Well, this is certainly a problem. You're interrupting my fishing. What was that you said? A letter? Just what kind of letter is it, and what does it have to do with me?"

Akechi was quite the unsociable man.

Growing a bit irritated, Samon blurted out. "Do you happen to know of a villain named Twenty Faces?"

"Ooh, Twenty Faces? You're saying Twenty Faces sent you a letter?" The master detective showed not the least bit of surprise and continued to stare at his fishing rod.

Left with no other choice, the old man read the entire announcement out loud and gave a detailed explanation of the treasures kept at Kusakabe's Castle.

"Ah, so you're the owner of that strange place, eh?" Finally interested, Akechi turned his gaze back to the man.

"That's right. Those ancient works of art are treasures worth more than my own life. Please, Mr. Akechi, save this old man. I beg you."

"And what exactly are you asking me to do?"

"Please come to my house at once. And then, if you will, protect my treasures."

"Did you turn that letter in to the police? I think notifying them first is the proper thing to do."

"I understand, and I know I shouldn't say this, but I trust you more than the police. I believe you are the only detective alive who can stand up to Twenty Faces. The only police station out here is a small substation, and it would take time to get reinforcements. Twenty Faces announced that he would invade my home tonight, so we can't exactly dawdle. It must be providence that brought you to this hot spring today, detective! Please, this is a once in a lifetime request. You must help me," Samon begged.

"Fine, if you insist, I'll take on the job. Twenty Faces is my enemy. So much so, in fact, that I've been waiting anxiously for him to reappear.

"Shall we return together, then? Or wait. Before that, we'll have to contact the police. I'll return to the inn and call them. Just in case, I think we should call two or three officers for backup," added Akechi. "You go on ahead of me. I'll be there soon with the police."

Akechi's voice revealed his excitement. He wasn't even glancing at the fishing rod anymore.

"Thank you, thank you so much! There's not a thing that could make me feel safer." Letting out a huge sigh of relief, Samon thanked Akechi over and over again.

18   A NIGHT OF DREAD

KUSAKABE SAMON TOOK A taxi home from Shūzenji back
to his castle in Taniguchi Village, and Akechi Kogorō arrived
thirty minutes later.

Aside from the detective himself, who was dressed in a tai-
lored black suit, there were three robust men in business suits.
They were police detectives assigned to the substation and introduced themselves to Samon with detailed business cards.

The elderly man immediately guided the quartet to the rear
art room. There, he explained one by one the histories of the
hanging scrolls covering the walls and the masterpieces filling
boxes on the shelves.

"Why, thank you, this is truly a stunning collection. I'm a
fan of ancient paintings myself, and often go to visit the trea-
suries of temples and museums when I have the chance, but
I've never seen so many historical treasures gathered in one
place like this.

"It's understandable why an art lover such as Twenty Faces
set his sights on this place. Even *I* may start drooling any minute now."

As if his wonder would never cease, detective Akechi paid
compliment after compliment to each piece. Even Samon was
surprised at his knowledge: the detective seemed to know
more than many art experts! The elderly man's respect for the
master detective grew.

After eating dinner a bit earlier than usual, the five men
began their work to protect the treasures.

Akechi ordered the three policemen briskly, sending one to the front entrance, one to the rear entrance, and stationing one in the art room itself. They were each to work through the night, whistling whenever they caught sight of something suspicious.

Once the policemen were in their places, detective Akechi had Samon close the sturdy wooden door to the art room and lock it.

"I'm going to sit in front of this door all night long and do my best," the master detective said, sitting down in the corridor outside the room.

"Are you sure it'll be all right, Mr. Akechi? I know this may sound rude, but our opponent is like a magician, after all. For some reason I've started to get a spooky feeling," the old man said awkwardly, studying Akechi's expression.

"Ha ha ha. There's nothing to worry about. I just checked everything over myself. There are tough steel bars on those windows, sturdy, thirty-centimeter thick walls, and a policeman on watch. On top of that, I myself am guarding the only entrance. We've taken all the precautions we can. You should just relax and go to bed. It won't make a difference whether you're standing here or not."

Samon found it hard to follow the detective's suggestion. "No, I'll stay all night here with you. Even if I tried to sleep, I wouldn't be able to, I fear." Saying this, he sat down next to the detective.

"I see. In that case, it's probably for the best. I'd rather have someone to talk to. How about discussing some art theory?" Not surprisingly, the veteran detective was relaxed to an irritating degree.

And so, the two got comfortable and talked on and off about classical paintings. Akechi did most of the talking, however, as Samon was fidgety and couldn't seem to settle down. He was hardly able to carry on a conversation. He felt that years had passed before midnight finally came. The night was now half over. From time to time, Akechi called over to the policeman behind the door, and he always answered right away, reporting that nothing was amiss.

"Ah, I'm a bit tired," Akechi yawned. "That Twenty Faces scoundrel might not come tonight after all. He's probably too wary to try and charge into such a heavily guarded place. How about a smoke, my good man? To help keep you awake. Overseas, they puff these luxurious ones all day long." Akechi opened his cigarette case with a snap, taking one for himself and then placing the container in front of Samon.

"I wonder. You really think he won't come tonight?" asked Samon, still jittery as he accepted the Egyptian tobacco.

"Nah, rest at ease. He won't do anything stupid, that's for sure. As long as he knows I'm here, he'll never just come waltzing in."

There was a lull in their conversation after that, and the two became lost in thought while enjoying their cigarettes.

Once the cigarettes had turned to ash, Akechi yawned again. "I'm going to get a little shuteye. You should too. Come now, there's nothing to worry about! They say true warriors awaken at the drop of a pin, remember? And this is my job, you know, so there's no creeping tiptoe I can't hear. I never fall completely asleep."

By the time he had finished talking, Akechi was lying down next to the wooden door with his eyes closed. Then the sound of his gentle rhythmic breathing could be heard.

In contrast to the relaxed behavior of the detective, Samon was becoming more and more antsy. Sleeping was the last thing on his mind; he was pricking his ears even more now, attempting to catch even the tiniest murmur. In fact, he thought he could almost hear a strange noise, but it could have just been tinnitus, or the wind blowing through the trees.

Listening even more closely, Samon sensed the night slipping deeper and deeper into silence. His mind gradually emptied, and a haze filled his eyes. The next thing he knew, the faint shape of a man in black with glowing eyes had appeared amid the fog.

"Ah, Mr. Akechi! The thief, the thief!" he suddenly screamed, shaking the sleeping Akechi's shoulder.

"What's that? You're just imagining things. I don't see any thief! You were just having a dream," he scolded, without moving an inch.

Was it only a dream? Or perhaps a hallucination? No matter where he looked afterwards, the man in black was nowhere to be found.

Feeling a bit ashamed, Samon returned to his original position in silence and tried listening intently once more. Just as before, his mind went blank, and fog gathered in front of his eyes.

The mist grew thicker, finally transforming into a black cloud. Feeling as if he were slipping deep, deep into the earth, Samon dozed off to sleep. For the duration of his slumber, Samon saw a succession of horrible nightmares, as if he had fallen to the underworld itself. Surprisingly enough, by the time he woke, his surroundings were bright with morning.

"Ah, I fell asleep, didn't I? But how could I have dozed off being so tense like that?" Samon was utterly puzzled.

Looking around, he spotted detective Akechi in the same position as before, sleeping soundly.

"Oh, what a relief. Twenty Faces really must have been too scared of detective Akechi to come after all. Thank heavens!"

Sighing in relief, Samon roused the detective. "Please wake up, Mr. Akechi. It's morning."

Akechi awoke immediately. "Ah, that was a good rest. Now look! Nothing happened, just as I told you," he said, stretching.

"The officer on watch must be very tired. It should be safe now, so let's give him some breakfast and then let him get some rest."

"Good idea. Please open this door, then."

Samon did as he was told, pulling the key out of his pocket and unlocking the door, then opening it with a rattle. But once the door was open and he could get a good look around the room a shriek burst from his throat, as if he were being strangled.

"What's wrong? What's wrong?" Akechi stood in surprise, and looked into the room. "Huh? What the—?"

Samon had no strength to speak. He merely babbled nonsense and touched the walls with shaking hands.

As he gazed over the room, Akechi understood the cause of the man's horror. Every single piece of art, whether it had been hanging on the wall or sealed in a box, had disappeared! The police detective was on the floor as if he had been knocked out, snoring at an embarrassingly loud volume.

"M-Mr. Akechi, th-th-they've been stolen! Ah, my, my. . ."

Samon's face was ghastly, as if he had instantly aged a decade, and he looked as if he were about to leap for Akechi's throat.

19 DEVILISH WISDOM

THE IMPOSSIBLE HAD HAPPENED yet again! And this time the nefarious Twenty Faces appeared not as a person but as an incorporeal phantom! As the fiend himself had said earlier, he made possible what no one else could.

Akechi walked briskly into the room and abruptly kicked the snoring police detective in the rear. Being caught unawares by the thief had drained the man completely of his good humor.

"Hey! Hey, wake up! I don't remember telling you to take a catnap in here! Look around—every single piece has been stolen!"

The policeman gradually picked himself up, still half-asleep. "Wh-wh-what was stolen, you say? Ah, I fell right asleep. Hey, where are we?" He gazed around the room with drowsy eyes.

"Get a grip on yourself. Ah, I've got it. You were knocked out with an anesthetic, weren't you? Think back, what did you do last night?" Akechi grabbed the man's shoulders and shook him wildly.

"Whoa, is that you, Mr. Akechi? Ah, this is the Kusakabe Art Fortress, isn't it? Yes, I was knocked out! And by an anesthetic, just like you said! In the middle of the night, a dark shadow crept behind me. Then he covered my nose and mouth with something soft that smelled funny! That's the last thing I can remember."

The police detective finally seemed to awaken and looked around the room apologetically.

"I thought so. I assume the men at the front and back gates met the same fate."

With this, Akechi left the room. After only a little while, he let out a loud shout from the kitchen.

"Mr. Kusakabe! Please come here!"

Wondering what was the matter, Samon and the police detective ran towards the voice. Akechi was standing at the entrance to the servants' room pointing inside. "I haven't found a trace of the policemen at the two exits. But that isn't all. Look for yourselves. . . The poor souls."

In a corner of the room, the butler Sakuzō and his wife were bound arms and legs and gagged. The thief had clearly gotten to them. To make sure they wouldn't cause him any trouble, he had immobilized the two elderly servants.

"What in the world? Mr. Akechi, what in the world happened here?" Kusakabe was nearly out of his mind by this point, clinging to Akechi's side. The treasures he valued more than his own life had all been stolen in a single night, so it was understandable.

"I can't begin to apologize for what happened here. To think that Twenty Faces was this skilled a thief. Underestimating my opponent was my true failure."

"Failure? Mr. Akechi, are you simply going to let this end in failure? What do you expect me to do now? A master detective! People call you a master detective, and yet look at what you've allowed to happen!" Samon's face turned pale as he glared at Akechi with bloodshot eyes, ready to lunge at the man.

Ashamed, Akechi hung his head. After a moment, he looked up, sporting a smile, of all things! This smile soon spread from ear to ear, until he began laughing loudly, as if the whole situation were unbearably hilarious.

Kusakabe Samon was dumbfounded. Utterly humiliated by his loss to the thief, had detective Akechi lost his mind? "What are you laughing about, Mr. Akechi? What's so funny?!"

"Wa ha ha ha! How is this *not* funny—the master detective Akechi Kogorō, suffering such a pathetic defeat? Easily, effortlessly foiled like an utter imbecile! Twenty Faces is truly a genius. I have to say, I respect him." Akechi seemed to be losing more and more of his sanity by the second.

"What? *What?* Mr. Akechi! What's come over you? This isn't the time to be complimenting your opponent! How despicable! But never mind that. Are you just going to leave poor Sakuzō and his wife like this? Snap to it, officer, and untie them at once! If we get those gags out of their mouths, they might be able to give us some clues about the thief."

Akechi was no longer the least bit dependable at this point, so the situation had completely reversed: it was now Kusakabe Samon, of all people, who was giving orders like a detective.

"You heard the man! Untie them," ordered Akechi, signaling the detective strangely with his eyes.

The previously groggy-looking police detective instantly leaped to his feet. With lightning speed, he pulled a police rope from his coat, spun Kusakabe around, and deftly tied the man's hands behind his back.

"Hey, what are you doing? Oh, so now you've all gone mad, eh? What are you tying me for, you nincompoops? I told you to release those two on the floor! Release me at once!"

The police detective showed no sign of loosening his grip. In fact, he did quite the opposite, silently restraining the old man's arms and legs.

"You maniac! Just what's gotten into you? Ow, that hurts! That hurts, I said! Mr. Akechi, what are you laughing at? Aren't you going to stop him? Mr. Akechi!" Samon could no longer comprehend what was happening. Had everyone really lost their sanity all at once? And if not, then what other reason could they have for tying up their own client? And what reason could a detective have for laughing at such a scene?

"Who are you calling for? It sounded like you said the name Akechi just now," Akechi said.

"What is this, some kind of sick joke? Please don't tell me you've forgotten your own name now, Mr. Akechi!"

"Me, forget my own name? Wait, are you saying that *I'm* Akechi Kogorō?" The detective's remarks were getting stranger and stranger.

"Why, of course I am! What is this madness?"

"Ha ha ha. Perhaps it is you who has gone mad, my good sir. After all, there isn't a soul named Akechi present now."

Hearing this, Samon's jaw dropped open, as if he were seeing a ghost. He was so overwhelmed, in fact, that he suddenly fell silent.

"Have you ever met Akechi Kogorō before, Mr. Kusakabe?"

"I've never met him, but I've seen his pictures numerous times."

"Pictures? I'm afraid pictures alone are a bit unreliable. Is this to say that I resemble the man you saw in those pictures?"

Mr. Kusakabe was speechless.

"Sounds to me like you forgot just what kind of a man Twenty Faces is, Mr. Kusakabe. Come now, you remember, don't you? Twenty Faces is a master of disguise."

"Th-then, that means you're...," Samon finally began to comprehend what was happening. And as he did, a look of terror appeared on his face.

"Ha ha ha. So you've finally figured it out."

"No... no... This can't be possible! I saw it in the newspaper! It said 'Akechi Kogorō's Homecoming' in the *Izu Daily*! And the woman at the Fujiya Inn led me to you. There couldn't have been any mistake!"

"And yet you made a colossal one. For Akechi Kogorō is still overseas."

"The newspaper wouldn't print a lie!"

"And yet they did. For a certain reporter in the local news department got misled by my scheme, and handed his editor a false manuscript."

"Hmph. But then what about the police detectives? There's no way the police would cover up for a fake detective Akechi!"

Samon simply didn't want to believe that the man standing in front of him was the fearsome Twenty Faces. He was determined to believe this man was Akechi Kogorō, no matter what.

"Ha ha ha. Still not convinced, sir? Maybe you should ask your doctor for a checkup. Police detectives? Ah, you must mean this man, and the other two at the exits. I just had my boys do a little impersonating, that's all."

But Samon wouldn't—no, couldn't—bring himself to believe it. The man he had believed to be Akechi Kogorō was not a master detective at all, but a master thief: the terrifying, hair-raising Fiend with Twenty Faces. And Twenty Faces was now standing before him!

Ah, what an unthinkable thought. The lead detective, of all people, turned out to be the thief. Kusakabe Samon had entrusted Twenty Faces himself with the job of protecting those valuable treasures!

"By the way, sir, did you enjoy that Egyptian cigarette last night? Ha ha ha. Remember now? I slipped a little drug in there. Then the two other police detectives went into that room and carried the goods out to my car. I wanted to make sure you got a good night's rest, you know. So now you want to know how I got inside? Ha ha ha. Why, it's elementary! I simply borrowed the key you put in your own pocket!"

Twenty Faces spoke mildly, as if he were talking about the weather. To Samon, the overly courteous nature of the man's speech was only the source of further outrage. "Anyway, we're in a bit of a hurry, so please excuse us. Rest assured that I will take excellent care of your treasures. Now then, I bid you a good day, sir."

Twenty Faces bowed politely, called together his disguised henchmen and departed.

Spouting unintelligible shrieks, Samon attempted to chase after the thief. The ends of the ropes binding him had been tied to a nearby pillar, so as soon as the man stood he immediately fell back down. And so Kusakabe Samon was left gnashing his teeth in sorrow and vexation, crying his eyes out as he continued to writhe in vain.

20 THE GIANT AND THE FIEND

TWO WEEKS AFTER THE incident at the Art Fortress, a lone boy came walking along a crowded Tokyo Station platform one afternoon. It was none other than detective Akechi's young assistant, Kobayashi Yoshio, with whom you're well acquainted by now. He wore a jacket and a dashing hunting cap; his shiny shoes clicked as he strode down the platform. He carried a rolled-up newspaper that featured a horrifying article on Twenty Faces. But allow me to save that story for a bit later.

Kobayashi had come to Tokyo Station with the sole intent of welcoming home Akechi Kogorō. This time, the master detective really was coming home from abroad. Akechi had been requested to take part in a big case in a foreign country, and was now coming home with another marvelous success under his belt, much like a triumphant general returning from

the battlefield. Normally, people from the Ministry of Foreign Affairs or other agencies would have come to welcome him, but Akechi had no taste for pomp. He preferred to keep a low profile because of his occupation, so he didn't announce his return, only telling his wife his scheduled arrival time at Tokyo Station. Mrs. Akechi seldom ventured out, so she had Kobayashi go in her stead.

Kobayashi glanced at his wristwatch repeatedly. In only five more minutes, Mr. Akechi would finally be returning home aboard a steam train. Kobayashi had not seen the detective in three months, and cherished memories were already causing him to tremble with excitement.

The next thing Kobayashi knew, a handsome gentleman approached him with a broad smile on his face. This gentleman was dressed in a mouse-colored, warm-looking overcoat and carried a staff made of wisteria. His salt-and-pepper hair matched his mustache of the same color on his fleshy face, and he wore gleaming tortoiseshell glasses. He was grinning at Kobayashi, yet the boy detective had never seen him before.

"Might you be Akechi's boy?" the gentleman asked with a gentle eye.

"Yes, but. . ."

Noting the boy's questioning look, the stranger introduced himself. "I'm Tsujino, from the Ministry of Foreign Affairs. I heard that Mr. Akechi would be returning on this train, so I came to welcome him unofficially. I also happen to have a personal request for him."

"Oh, is that so? I'm Mr. Akechi's assistant, Kobayashi."

Seeing the boy remove his hat and bow, Mr. Tsujino smiled again. "Yes, I've heard of you. And I recalled seeing your face in a newspaper photograph, so that's why I approached you. Your face-off against Twenty Faces was truly marvelous! And you've earned quite a reputation for yourself, to boot. All of my children are huge Kobayashi fans, you know," he laughed, praising the lad.

Kobayashi blushed.

"Speaking of Twenty Faces, I heard he recently had the audacity to impersonate Mr. Akechi at Shūzenji. And just in yesterday's paper, it said that he was planning to rob the national museum! It's really shocking how he's made fools of the police. We absolutely cannot let this man run free any longer. I've been waiting desperately for Mr. Akechi's return, if only because I believe he has what it takes to crush that fiend once and for all."

"Yes, me too. I tried my best, but I suppose I was a little out of my league. I've been waiting expectantly for Mr. Akechi, hoping he would come home soon and take revenge for me."

"Is that yesterday's newspaper?"

"Yes. It has the notice by Twenty Faces stating he's going to rob the national museum," replied Kobayashi, opening the paper to the page and showing the article. Articles about Twenty Faces were splattered across the local news section because of the special delivery letter he had sent to the curator of the national museum the previous day. The letter contained a shocking notice by Twenty Faces that he intended to take every last work of art from the museum's vaults! It also specified the date of the theft: December 10—only nine days away.

It seemed the appalling ambition of the Fiend with Twenty Faces had reached its zenith. Regardless of the details, Twenty Faces clearly intended to take on the entire nation this time. Every location he had targeted until now had been owned by a private entity, and while his acts were indeed abhorrent, they were not exactly unheard of. Burglarizing the national museum, however, meant the theft of national property—something that no thief, no matter how brazen, had ever attempted in the history of Japan. Words like daring or reckless no longer sufficed—this thief was a monster.

But was such a feat actually possible? Dozens of government officials were employed at the national museum. It had its own security team as well as police. On top of that, the thief had announced when he would come knocking, so it was anyone's guess just how tight the surveillance would be. It was possible that they would simply surround the entire complex with a ring of policemen.

Had Twenty Faces completely lost his mind? Or did he truly possess the confidence to complete this absolutely impossible mission? Then again this was a devil who had proved time and time again that he was fully capable of carrying out plans that defied human imagination.

Now then, we must leave the Twenty Faces matter at this, Intrepid Reader, for it's time to welcome home detective Akechi.

"Oh, the train's coming," Mr. Tsujino said, but Kobayashi had already run to the edge of the platform. Standing at the front of the crowd of welcoming people and looking over his left shoulder, Kobayashi could see Mr. Akechi's train loom larger with each passing moment.

A blast of wind shot by, followed by black train cars. Faces of passengers could be seen through the windows, until the train finally came to a halt with a squeal of its brakes. Then, from the first-class entryway, the sorely missed Mr. Akechi appeared. Dressed all in black, with a black business suit, a black overcoat, and a black felt hat, he soon noticed Kobayashi, smiled and waved.

"Welcome home!" Filled with happiness, Kobayashi ran to his mentor's side. Detective Akechi handed numerous trunks to the porter and then stepped down to the platform and approached the boy.

"Seems like you had a lot of work on your hands while I was gone, Kobayashi. I read all about it in the papers. It's wonderful to see that you're all right."

Ah, his mentor's voice for the first time in three months. With his gaze locked on the master detective, Kobayashi approached him and the two exchanged a firm handshake.

Just then, Mr. Tsujino walked over to Akechi and offered his business card. "Mr. Akechi? We've never met, but I'm Mr. Tsujino from the Ministry of Foreign Affairs. I heard about your arrival from a certain source, so I came with the intention of discussing a classified matter with you."

Akechi accepted the business card, and stared at it intently for a moment. Then, as if something had suddenly occurred to him he said cheerfully, "Ah, Mr. Tsujino. Is that so? I'm quite familiar with your name. Actually, once I got home and changed my clothes, I was planning to head over to the Ministry of Foreign Affairs at once. But I'm quite honored that you took time out of your busy schedule to come and welcome me."

"I know you must be tired, but if you have no objections, I'd like to sit down for a cup of tea with you in the nearby Railroad Hotel. I promise not to take too much of your time."

"The Railroad Hotel? I see. The Railroad Hotel. . ." Akechi stared at Mr. Tsujimo then whispered something with an intrigued look on his face. "No, I haven't the slightest objection," he said. "Allow me to accompany you."

Akechi then approached Kobayashi, who was waiting a few steps away. "Kobayashi, I'm going to stop by the hotel with that fellow over there, so take my luggage in a taxi and go home ahead of me, would you?" he said in a low voice.

"Yes, sir. Then I'll be on my way now." Kobayashi followed the porter.

The master detective watched the boy head off and then fell into step with Mr. Tsujino, speaking to him as if they were old friends. The two took a pedestrian underpass below the tracks then walked to the hotel above the station.

Mr. Tsujino had apparently reserved a room on the hotel's top floor. A headwaiter with a fine physique respectfully ushered them in. The two men sat down at a round table draped in an extravagant cloth and eased into the comfortable chairs. Another waiter came in carrying tea and cakes, as if he had been waiting for this moment.

"Now then, we have some private discussing to do, so please leave us be. I'll ring the bell if I need you, so don't let anyone else in," Mr. Tsujino ordered, and the waiter exited with a bow.

Alone, the two men stared at each other.

"Mr. Akechi, I can't begin to tell you how much I've wanted to meet you. Every moment I spent waiting seemed like an eternity." Mr. Tsujino smiled fondly. His eyes, however, remained focused on Akechi.

Akechi let his body sink into the soft cushion of the chair and replied equally cheerfully, "On the contrary, if only I could describe how eager I was to meet with you! In fact, as I was riding the train, I had just gotten to thinking: with any luck he'll come to the station to welcome me home."

"I would expect no less from the master detective. In that case, I assume you know my true name?" A powerful force lurked behind Mr. Tsujino's casual question, and his left hand began to tremble on the chair's armrest.

"I knew you weren't Mr. Tsujino from the Ministry of Foreign Affairs the moment I saw that seemingly genuine business card of yours. As for your true name, I'm afraid it eludes me, but the newspapers refer to you as the Fiend with Twenty Faces." Akechi relayed this shocking truth in a composed voice.

Oh, Intrepid Reader, could this really be the truth? The thief, coming to welcome the detective home? And despite knowing this, the detective still allowed himself to be invited to enjoy a cup of tea by his foe! How could such a mind-boggling scenario come to pass?

"You're exactly the man I imagined you to be, Akechi. Realizing who I was the minute you saw me, yet still complying with my request. I doubt even Sherlock Holmes himself would be capable of pulling off such a feat. Really, I'm quite amused. What a splendid day this is! This moment of excitement alone is enough to make me feel thankful to be alive!"

It almost sounded as if Twenty Faces was venerating detective Akechi, but letting his guard down was out of the question. This disguised creature was a master thief who had made an enemy of the entire country. All of the ventures this villain undertook were practically suicide missions, so thorough preparation was of the utmost importance. See for yourself, Intrepid Reader. Mr. Tsujino's right hand had been inside his pocket from the beginning of the mission and had yet to move. Just what could he be gripping?

"Ha ha ha. It seems you're a little too excited, if you ask me. This situation isn't the least bit unusual for me. Although, Twenty Faces, I do pity you a tad. You see, now that I've returned, that master plan you've gone to such lengths to achieve is going to be utterly ruined, and you won't even be able to lay a hand on the artwork in the museum. I won't let you keep Kusakabe's treasures either, understand? That I promise." Akechi also looked quite jovial as he spoke. He blew a deep puff of smoke straight into his opponent's face and grinned from ear to ear.

"Well, then, allow me to make a promise as well." Twenty Faces did not back down. "I will steal every last piece from the museum on the scheduled day, right in front of your very eyes. And as for Kusakabe's treasures, do you really think you can get those back from me? Don't forget now, Akechi, you yourself were an accomplice in the crime!"

"An accomplice? Oh, I see. You certainly have a unique sense of humor!"

Determined to bring the other to ruin, both men burned with deep animosity as they exchanged a friendly chat like old chums. Neither lowered his guard in the slightest.

Akechi knew just how foolhardy Twenty Faces was, so there was no telling what the thief had prepared behind the scenes. The pistol in Twenty Faces' pocket wasn't the only thing Akechi feared. The peculiar headwaiter might possibly have been one of the villain's henchmen as well. And who knew how many toadies lay in wait throughout the hotel.

The way both men sat facing each other now was exactly the way two trained swordsmen would square off against each other with unsheathed blades. It was a battle of wills that would be decided by the slightest indiscretion.

Both men began to speak with even more amiability. Despite the cold weather, beads of sweat began to trickle down their foreheads. Their eyes, however, glowed brighter and brighter like blazing flames.

21 Trunk & Elevator

IF MASTER DETECTIVE AKECHI Kogorō had wished to capture the thief when they met at the platform, there would have been nothing to it. Why on earth would he have let such a perfect chance slip away? Intrepid Reader, I understand your perplexity.

It demonstrates just how much confidence the detective had in himself; he was able to make such a shocking decision because he knew he was the smarter one. Akechi was positive that under his watch, he would be able to return the numerous works of art to Kusakabe's Castle *and* keep the villain from laying a finger on the national museum's artifacts.

And arresting the thief now would put him at a disadvantage. Twenty Faces had many henchmen. If their leader were out of the picture, there was no telling how his men would dispose of the stolen goods. He had to find out where those priceless valuables were hidden first.

So instead of disappointing the thief, who had come to welcome him, Akechi found it much more amusing to pretend to accept the man's invitation and then confirm just how naïve the villain really was.

"Akechi, go ahead and imagine the position I'm in right now. If you wanted to arrest me, you could do so at any time. Look, all you need to do is push that bell there and order the waiter to call the police. Ha ha ha. What a fine adventure this is! Can you understand this thrill? I'm risking my life here! At this very moment, I'm standing at the brink of a precipice above a bottomless abyss!"

Twenty Faces was entirely fearless. As he spoke, he narrowed his eyes and scrutinized the detective's face, laughing like a hyena.

Akechi Kogorō laughed in response. "Come now, there's no reason to be that afraid, you poor fool. Seeing that you've come all the way out here despite my knowing who you really are, I don't feel at all like arresting you. I really just wanted to have a conversation with the famous Twenty Faces, plain and simple. I mean, there's no reason to rush to arrest you, is there? Why, there're still nine whole days left until you visit the museum! I'm going to relax, take my time, and watch your futile efforts right down to the very end."

"Oh, that's my master detective, all right! You truly are a bold man. I really admire you now. By the way, since it seems you're not going to capture me, that gives me an opportunity to capture you instead, now doesn't it?" As the tone of Twenty Faces' voice gradually rose, his smirk twisted more and more diabolically. "Aren't you afraid, Akechi? Don't tell me you think I brought you all the way here for no reason. Do you think I haven't prepared a little surprise? That I'd just scoot you outside without another word once we finished our business? It seems you've misunderstood things a bit."

"I wonder. Of course I plan to leave here when I like, regardless of whether you try to stop me. I'm rather busy, you know, and as I said, I have to stop by the Ministry of Foreign Affairs." As he spoke, Akechi stood and walked in the opposite direction of the door. He gazed outside as if admiring the view. Yawning slightly, the detective pulled out a handkerchief and wiped his brow.

At that moment, the brawny headwaiter strode into the room along with another muscular boy, answering some unheard call. Both stood at attention in front of the table.

"Tsk tsk, Akechi. It seems as though you still haven't fathomed the scope of my abilities. Don't go relaxing just because this is the Railroad Hotel. Allow me to demonstrate," Twenty

Faces said, glancing toward the two big men. "Go introduce yourselves to Mr. Akechi." Instantly, the duo snarled and plunged ahead with their eyes locked on the detective.

"Wait just a moment. What do you think you're doing?" Akechi turned his back to the window and assumed a defensive posture.

"Still don't understand, hmm? Fine. Then take a look at your feet. There's a trunk sitting there that's a little too large for me to carry on my own, isn't there? Well, it's empty, and guess who's going to fill it? My boys here are going to shut you up inside that trunk! Ha ha ha! I imagine even the master detective himself must be a little surprised. It never crossed your mind that my subordinates would have infiltrated the hotel staff, did it?

"No, no, calling for help won't do you any good here. You see, I reserved the rooms on either side of this one. And these two men you see before you aren't the only people I've planted here. I have watchmen stationed in the hallways just to make sure we are not interrupted."

Oh, what a slip-up! Our master detective had fallen into the enemy's trap. Despite knowing exactly what was going on, he had leaped out of the frying pan and into the fire. If Twenty Faces had been this careful in his preparations, then there was surely no escape.

Now, remember that Twenty Faces hated blood. He was most likely not planning to actually take his opponent's life. But this *was* Akechi Kogorō, a man who posed more of a danger to the thief than the police department itself. Twenty Faces was most likely planning to put the detective into the trunk, transport him to a place where no one could find him, and then imprison him until the theft at the national museum had been finished.

Deaf to Akechi's appeals, the two large men closed in on the detective. They seemed to hesitate a bit, despite looking ready to pounce on him at any second. The power emanating from Akechi had struck them.

Two—or in this case, three—men could always overpower one, so no matter how strong Akechi Kogorō was, that alone would not save him. Who would have believed that he would become a prisoner of the master thief so soon after returning home? Was Akechi truly fated to undergo such utter humiliation? Oh, say not so!

Keep your eyes sharp, Intrepid Reader. You see, even in this crisis, Akechi still wore that smile of his. Then, as if that smile was simply too strange to stay focused on, his assailants' momentum began to wane.

"Ha ha ha."

The two waiters stopped in their tracks, their mouths gaping open as if they were possessed.

"Oh, enough with the bravado, Akechi. What's so funny? Or are you so scared that you've lost your wits?" Unable to perceive his enemy's true intentions, Twenty Faces had no choice but to keep taunting him.

"Oh, so sorry, please excuse me. It's just hilarious watching you all acting so dramatic and serious. Would you mind coming over here for a second? Look out this window here for me. You'll see something unusual."

"Something unusual? Like what? The only thing visible from there is the roof of the train station! How pathetic! The great Akechi Kogorō, trying to buy time with some silly bluff!" The thief seemed somewhat concerned about the man's claim, however, and couldn't keep from approaching the window.

"Ha ha ha. Of course there's nothing but the roof. But there's something unusual beyond it. Look over there." Akechi pointed. "In between this roof and the one over there, there's something in black hunched over. Do you see it? It looks like a child. And he seems to be looking this way with a telescope, of all things! Now doesn't his face look a little familiar to you?"

Intrepid Reader, I'm sure you've already figured out who this mystery boy was. That's right: it was detective Akechi's assistant, Kobayashi, just as you guessed! Using one of his seven tools, the pen telescope, he was peering into the hotel's window and waiting for a sign.

"Kobayashi, that little brat! So he didn't go home after all."

"That's right. I told him to check at the hotel's front desk to see what room I went to and then watch the window."

The thief hadn't grasped exactly what that meant, though. "So what?" Growing more and more anxious, Twenty Faces approached Akechi in a threatening manner.

"Look at this. Look in my hand. Whatever happens to me, my handkerchief will surely flutter out this window."

Indeed, Akechi had slipped his right hand out the window, which was slightly ajar, and was dangling a white handkerchief from his fingers. "This is my signal. Once he sees this, that boy will hop off the platform and dash into the station office. The alarm will sound. Then the police will come running and secure the entrances and exits to the hotel. Wouldn't you agree that five minutes would be more than enough time for that to happen? And I know I possess the strength to hold you three off for five or ten minutes. How's that? Shall I let go of the handkerchief? If I do, at least I'll get to see the spectacle of the great Twenty Faces finally getting arrested."

Looking from the handkerchief to Kobayashi on the train platform, the thief thought frantically for a moment. In the end, as he recognized his disadvantageous situation, his gaze softened.

"So, then am I to believe that if I allow you to leave in one piece, you will *not* drop that handkerchief? In other words, I exchange your freedom for mine."

"Of course. As I stated earlier, I have no intention of arresting you now. If I had, I wouldn't have bothered with this handkerchief signal in the first place. I'd just have sent Kobayashi straight to the police. Just think. If I had, you'd be stewing in a jail cell by now!"

"Your actions truly puzzle me. You really want to let me get away that much?"

"Indeed. I feel it'd be a waste if I simply captured you easily now. Someday, I *will* get my hands on not only you but your legion of henchmen as well as all the stolen art you've amassed until now, all at once. But maybe I'm getting a little too greedy."

Twenty Faces bit his lip in outraged silence for a long moment. Then, as if he had suddenly had a change of heart, the thief's smile returned. "I would expect no less from Akechi Kogorō. That's the way you must be. Don't be offended. I just felt like toying with you a little, that's all. I wasn't serious by any means. Now then, let's call it a day, and I'll see you to the door."

But the detective was not so gullible as to get trapped by such a duplicitous offer. "Oh, I'm all for leaving, but I can't seem to take my eyes off those waiters of yours. Suppose you send them, along with your watchmen in the corridors, to the kitchen?"

Twenty Faces didn't hesitate and immediately ordered his henchmen to leave. The door to the room was left wide open, giving Akechi an ample view of the corridor.

"How's that? Listen, you can hear their footsteps going down the stairs."

Akechi finally left the window and put his handkerchief back into his pocket. There's no way the entire Railroad Hotel could be commandeered by Twenty Faces, so as long as he made it into the corridor, he thought he would be fine. It seemed that there were guests in other rooms as well, which meant the corridors in those areas weren't controlled by the thief and had real waiters walking around in them.

Once again shoulder to shoulder like old friends, the two men walked to the elevator. A uniformed elevator boy around twenty years old was waiting patiently by the open doors. As

Akechi casually stepped in, he heard, "Ah, I forgot my cane. You go on ahead."

As soon as Twenty Faces said this, the doors closed shut behind Akechi, and the elevator began its descent. "This is fishy," Akechi quickly realized. Staying calm, he closely watched the hands of the elevator boy. Just as he had surmised, the elevator came to a jarring stop once it reached the walled-in interval between the first and second floors.

"What's wrong?"

"Sorry, sir. It looks like the elevator's malfunctioned. Just a moment—it'll be fixed soon," the boy said apologetically as he repeatedly tinkered with the machinery.

"What are you doing? Out of the way," Akechi said sharply, grabbing the boy by the scruff of his neck and pulling him away. He pulled with such force, in fact, that the boy tumbled backwards into a corner of the elevator. "It's no use trying to fool me. You think I don't know how elevators work?"

Akechi gripped the handle tightly and then twisted it. Amazingly, the elevator continued down to the first floor with no difficulty. Once it had descended, Akechi turned around to stare daggers at the boy, keeping his grip on the handle. And, oh, the terror those eyes wrought! The young man began quaking and pressed on his right pocket as if something important were hidden there.

The clever detective didn't miss that. He pounced on the boy, dug his hand into the pocket, and snatched out a single bill. It was a thousand-yen note. The elevator boy had been bought by Twenty Faces for a mere thousand yen.

While Akechi was trapped in the elevator, the thief tried to escape incognito. No matter how fearless Twenty Faces might have been, he didn't possess the courage to walk alongside the detective through the crowded hotel entrance now that his identity was known. Akechi may have said he didn't intend to arrest the thief, but as a criminal, he dared not believe that.

The master detective bolted out of the elevator, bounded across the corridor and headed for the entrance. He was just in time: Twenty Faces was calmly walking down the stone steps in the guise of Mr. Tsujino.

"Oh, sorry to keep you waiting. The elevator had a slight malfunction, so getting down took some time." Akechi clapped Mr. Tsujino on the shoulder, smiling as he spoke.

If only you could have seen, Intrepid Reader, the look on Mr. Tsujino's face after turning around with a start and seeing Akechi right behind him. The thief had been convinced that his elevator plan would be a success, so it's understandable that an expression of complete stupefaction appeared on his face.

"Is something wrong, Mr. Tsujino? You don't look well. Oh, by the way, that elevator boy asked me to give this to you. He said he's sorry, but since your target knew how to operate an elevator, he wasn't able to stop it for as long as you had ordered." Akechi gleefully waved the bill in front of Mr. Tsujino's face a few times before placing it in his hands, laughing all the while. "I'll be on my way now. See you again soon," he said, spinning around and leaving without a single glance back.

Clutching the thousand-yen note, Twenty Faces watched the master detective walk off in a state of shock. He clicked his tongue in annoyance and called for a car that had been waiting off to the side.

And so, the first battle between the master thief and master detective ended in Akechi Kogorō's victory. The thief had been treated like a small fry that the detective could arrest whenever he wanted, and to the great Twenty Faces, there was no greater disgrace.

"I'll get you for this! Just wait!" Twenty Faces shook his fists at Akechi's back, muttering curses as the detective disappeared.

22   THE ARREST OF TWENTY FACES

"MI-MISTER AKECHI! I WAS just about to come see you. Where's the suspect?"

Before he had gotten even fifty meters from the Railroad Hotel, detective Akechi was stopped by a voice calling his name.

"Ah, Imanishi!" It was Detective Imanishi from the criminal investigations section of the Metropolitan Police Department.

"Save the greetings for later. What happened to the man calling himself Tsujino? You didn't let him get away, did you?"

"How do you know about that?"

"I found Kobayashi acting suspicious on the platform. He's really stubborn, you know. No matter how many times I asked him to tell me what was up, he wouldn't give me an answer. I changed my strategy, though, and finally got him to explain. He told me you had gone into the Railroad Hotel with a man from the Ministry of Foreign Affairs named Tsujino, who was actually, of all things, Twenty Faces in disguise! I called the ministry at once, and they said that Tsujino was right in his office, meaning the one with you had to be an impostor. That's when I came running over here to assist you."

"Good work, officer. But I'm afraid the man's already left."

"Left? So it wasn't Twenty Faces?'

"It was him. Today was my first time to meet him face to face, and I must say he's an interesting man. He's a worthy opponent in every respect."

"Mr. Akechi! Is this some kind of joke? You're saying you knew it was Twenty Faces, yet you didn't call the police and let him get away?" Aghast, Detective Imanishi began to question Akechi's sanity.

"I have a little plan," Akechi answered simply.

"A little plan? You can't just go and decide things on your own like that! No matter the circumstances, once you know he's the criminal, you cannot let him escape! My duty as an officer requires me to pursue him at all costs. Now where did he go? Did he leave by car?" Imanishi was indignant at how this ordinary citizen had handled the matter.

"If you want to pursue him, you're free to do so, but I'm afraid you won't get anywhere."

"I'm not taking orders from you. I'm going to go to the hotel, get the plates on that car, and then arrange a search."

"Oh, if it's the license plate number you want, you needn't go all the way to the hotel. It's 1-3-8-8-7."

"What? You even know the car's plate number? Then why in the world didn't you follow him?" Detective Imanishi was dumbfounded yet again but in this crisis couldn't afford to waste time on needless questions. Writing down the plate number in his notebook, he dashed to a police box a little ways ahead.

He made a phone call, and the news soon traveled to every police box and station in the city in the blink of an eye.

"Pursue and stop number 13887 at once! Inside is Twenty Faces disguised as Mr. Tsujino from the Ministry of Foreign Affairs."

Just think how surprised the policemen of Tokyo were when they heard this order. I shouldn't need to tell you how every officer in every police station became vigilant, their minds filled with images of the glory they would gain by capturing such a wanted criminal.

Twenty minutes after the villain had left the hotel, an officer stationed at the Totsukamachi police box in Shinjuku had the good fortune of spotting license plate number 13887. He was a young policeman brimming with courage. When a single car

sped past the police box clearly going over the speed limit, he glanced at its plate and saw those five numbers.

Shaking with adrenalin, the young policeman leaped into the traffic and stopped a car behind number 13887 and climbed inside. "Follow that car! The infamous Twenty Faces is in it! Go! Drive as fast as you want. Work that engine!" he screamed.

Fortunately, the driver of the car was also a young man, and the car a new one with a powerful engine. The driver revved it and accelerated, and they shot through the traffic.

The two racing automobiles did not go unnoticed by pedestrians. In the rear car, they could see a single policeman bent over the front seat, shouting, eyes locked on the automobile ahead of him.

"A chase! A chase!" Rubberneckers ran after the cars. Dogs howled, and passersby stopped to gaze in wonder. The two automobiles left everything behind as they raged ahead like demons. Just how many cars had they passed? Time after time they seemed sure to crash, just barely avoiding collisions with other cars in their way.

Since not much speed can be gained on narrow streets, the thief's car drove out onto the big loop line, rocketing toward Ōji. Obviously, he realized he was being chased, but there was nothing he could do. In the middle of the afternoon in the city, jumping out of a car and hiding was an impossible task.

Once they passed Ikebukuro, a loud bang sounded from the car in front. Had the thief finally lost all his patience and pulled that pistol from his pocket?

No, no, that wasn't what happened. What do you think this is, a mobster movie? Pulling out a pistol in a busy city like this wouldn't help him escape one bit.

The sound came from not a pistol but a blowout. Twenty Faces' luck had run out. Despite what happened, the car still moved ahead but soon lost its momentum. By that time, the police car had already passed it. The car swerved to the side, leaving the thief with nowhere to run.

Both automobiles came to a stop. A crowd gathered and policemen arrived.

Well, Intrepid Reader, it looked as if Mr. Tsujino had finally been captured.

"It's Twenty Faces! Twenty Faces!" cried the onlookers.

The thief was surrounded by two policemen and the young officer from Totsukamachi. As they pounced on him, Twenty Faces hung his head in shame, no longer able to resist.

"Twenty Faces has been captured!"

"What a shameless mug he's got!"

"But how about that policeman? What a guy!"

"Three cheers for the officer!"

The policeman dragged the thief through the clamoring crowd, stuffed him into the patrol car and hurried back to the police station.

Once they reached headquarters, the facts of the matter were established, and cheers resounded throughout the station. The elusive criminal who had caused Tokyo's police so much trouble had finally been captured, and rather easily at that! It was all thanks to Detective Imanishi's quick handling and the perseverance of the young officer from Totsukamachi. The two men gained such favor among their colleagues that they were almost paraded around the office on the shoulders of the other men.

Chief Inspector Nakamura was happier than anyone else after hearing the report. Ever since he had had the wool pulled over his eyes during the Hashiba incident, he had burned with resentment towards Twenty Faces.

The interrogation began at once. Because they were dealing with a master of disguise no one knew his true face. So the first thing they had to do was call in a witness to confirm the arrested man's identity.

Nakamura phoned the home of Akechi Kogorō. The master detective was at the Ministry of Foreign Affairs, so Kobayashi came in his stead.

In no time at all, the apple-cheeked boy arrived at the grim interrogation chamber. And as soon as he laid eyes on the thief, the boy testified that this Mr. Tsujino was indeed the impostor.

23 I'm Just Me!

"THIS IS THE MAN. Without a doubt," Kobayashi answered clearly.

"Ha ha ha. How's that for you? Foiled by a child! Now it won't matter what kind of excuse you make. You must be Twenty Faces!" Nakamura was elated at finally capturing his sworn enemy. He spoke in a triumphant voice and glared at the villain.

"Except I'm not. Oh, what a mess this is. I had no idea that he was the famous Twenty Faces, you know." Apparently, the disguised thief was still intent on acting innocent and began bluffing.

"What's that? You're not making any sense."

"Well, it doesn't make any sense to me either, but I think he disguised himself as me and then used me as a double."

"That's enough! We're not going to fall for this act no matter how many times you try it, bub!"

"No, really, this isn't an act. Please, just calm down and listen to my explanation. Here's who I am. And I'm certainly not Twenty Faces," the gentleman said, pulling out a business card case as if he had suddenly remembered it. The name "Matsushita Shōbei" was written on it along with the address of an apartment in Suginami.

"My name's Matsushita, just as it says here. I had a business failure a while back, and as I'm still unemployed, I live alone in that apartment. Anyway, yesterday as I was walking in Hibiya Park, I made the acquaintance of someone who appeared to be a businessman. He then approached me about a peculiar money-making venture.

"I was to ride around in a taxi for an entire day. The fare would be paid for, and on top of that I would get five thousand yen for the job. Now does that sound like a good deal or what? I know how I must look, but I'm actually unemployed, so five thousand was worth it to me.

"The man said there was a special purpose behind this job and began going on about some tedious matter. I stopped him, though, saying that the details didn't matter to me, and I'd be happy to take the job at once. So, I've been riding around here and there in that taxi since morning. I was told to have lunch at the Railroad Hotel, which I'm sure you can understand was a very welcome order. I filled my stomach then sat there for about thirty minutes, I think, until a man came out of the Railroad Hotel and got into my taxi.

"When I first saw him, my heart nearly jumped into my throat. I thought I had gone mad! From his face, to his suit, to his overcoat, right down to his cane—the man who got into the taxi looked exactly like me! It was like looking into a mirror—truly bizarre!

"As I watched in shock, I saw something even weirder. Right after he got into my taxi, he opened the door on the opposite side and hopped right out! Some gentleman who looked exactly like me just passed through the taxi, nothing more. Then he moved past me and said something strange: 'Please leave at once. It doesn't matter where you go, but drive at full speed.' You know that barbershop under the station? After he said that he slipped right into it. And my car was parked right in front of the entrance.

"It did seem a bit strange to me, but I had promised to follow through with this after all, so I got in and ordered the driver to go full speed ahead. I don't really remember where else I went after that, but I noticed a car following us about the time we reached the area behind Waseda University. For some reason I got really scared and kept shouting at the driver to speed up.

"Anyway, I'm sure you all know what happened then. And judging from what you said, it seems that I was tricked into becoming a double for Twenty Faces for five thousand yen. No, maybe not a double. I guess I'm the real one, and he's my double. He duplicated my face and clothes right down to the last detail, as if he were a walking photograph."

Matsushita concluded his account and then pulled strongly on his face and hair, even twisting his cheeks a bit. "And as proof, look at this. See? I'm the authentic Matsushita Shōbei. I'm the real one, and he's the fake! Now, did any of that make any sense?"

Oh, what a travesty! Chief Inspector Nakamura had once again been taken for a ride by Twenty Faces. The Metropolitan Police Department's joy at catching this heinous criminal had been premature after all. After calling in the landlord of the apartment Mr. Matsushita lived in, they confirmed the man's story.

What an assiduous scoundrel that Twenty Faces was! He had gone to such lengths just to attack detective Akechi at Tokyo Station. Infiltrating the Railroad Hotel with his subordinates, buying off the elevator boy, preparing his double Matsushita: his preparations for a smooth escape had been flawless.

To say the thief had found a double, though, would be a bit off the mark. For a man like Twenty Faces, there was absolutely no need to search around for a man who resembled himself. He was a fearsome master of disguise, after all. He could transform himself into any person he happened to get his hands on, making everything much simpler. Any average person walking down the street was a potential target. All he needed to do was find a simple soul gullible enough to fall for his sugar-coated words. And this unemployed gentleman known as Matsushita had been the perfect carefree, happy-go-lucky pawn.

24   Twenty Faces' New Recruit

AKECHI KOGORŌ'S HOUSE WAS in a quiet neighborhood in Ryūdochō, in Minato Ward. The master detective lived modestly with his beautiful young wife Fumiyo; his assistant, Kobayashi; and a maid.

It was evening by the time detective Akechi returned home after stopping by the Ministry of Foreign Affairs and then a friend's house. Kobayashi had just returned from the Metropolitan Police Department as well. He ran to Akechi's study on the second floor of the western-style house to report the details of the incident concerning Twenty Faces' double.

"I thought that was probably the case. I feel bad for Nakamura, though." The master detective grimaced.

"There's something I still don't understand, though, Mr. Akechi." Kobayashi was in the habit of asking questions whenever something didn't make sense to him. "I understand why you let Twenty Faces get away, but why didn't you let me follow him then? Don't we need to find out where his hideout is? Especially if we want to stop his attack on the museum."

Detective Akechi smiled as he listened to Kobayashi's criticism. Then he stood and moved over to the window, waving to the boy.

"Because he's going to tell me himself. And do you know why? Because I just embarrassed him a great deal back at that hotel not even attempting to arrest him, then letting him run off like that. You can't possibly imagine the degree of humiliation he suffered as a result.

"Just because of that one incident, Twenty Faces probably already hates me enough to kill me. On top of that, as long as I'm around, he's not going to be able to do as he pleases, so he's most likely thinking of a way to get rid of me as we speak.

"Look out this window. See that man over there telling a story with picture cards? Now, I ask you, who in their right mind would come out to such a lonely place and expect to draw a crowd for a show like that? He's been standing in the same spot for some time now, stealing glances at this window."

Kobayashi looked down on the narrow road in front of the gate to Akechi's house, and sure enough, there was a very suspicious-looking man telling a story with picture cards.

"He must be one of Twenty Faces' henchmen, then. He's come to see what you're up to, Mr. Akechi."

"That's right. There's no need for us to waste time and effort searching for him, because he's come straight to us. All we need to do is follow that man down there, and we'll find out where Twenty Faces' hideout is."

"I'll disguise myself and follow him then," Kobayashi said.

"There's no need for that. I have a plan. Remember, our opponent is a very sharp fellow, so we mustn't do anything thoughtless.

"By the way, Kobayashi, something a bit strange may happen to me tomorrow. You mustn't be surprised, though. I won't let Twenty Faces get the best of me, no matter what. Even if some sort of danger befalls me, it'll all be part of my plan, so you mustn't worry yourself. Understood?"

After hearing such a serious order, Kobayashi couldn't help but worry. "Mr. Akechi, if it's something dangerous, then please let me do it. It would be terrible if something were to happen to you."

"Thank you," Akechi said, patting the boy's shoulder. "But this isn't a job for you. Trust me. You know me better than anyone else. Have I ever failed to solve a case? There's no need to worry. Absolutely none."

IT HAPPENED THE NEXT evening.

The picture-card storyteller who had been standing in front of Akechi's house the day before had been replaced by a mumbling beggar imploring passers-by.

A filthy cloth was wrapped around his face, and he wore a ragged, patched kimono. Seated on a small mat, he seemed to be shivering due to the cold and looked quite pathetic.

Strangely enough, as fewer people came and went, the beggar's appearance underwent a great change. His drooping head rose and sharp eyes began to shine in his unshaven face, gazing intently at detective Akechi's house.

Detective Akechi had gone out at noon, but he returned three hours later. Seemingly unaware of the beggar keeping watch from the road, he went straight to his study, overlooking the front garden, and began writing something at his desk in front of the window. The beggar could see his every move.

The beggar waited patiently until evening, and detective Akechi also continued to sit patiently where he could be seen.

He received not a single visitor in the afternoon, but come night, a strange man walked through the low stone gate of his estate. The man had long, unkempt hair, and his face was buried in a wild beard. He was wearing a knitted shirt over a dirty business suit and a hunting cap so beat-up that it had lost its shape. Whether a vagrant or a tramp, he looked to be a bizarre fellow. Just after he entered the gate, a bloodcurdling yell resounded.

"Get out here, Akechi! I know you haven't forgotten my face yet, you shyster! I came to thank you for what you did for me! C'mon now, open up! I wanna thank you and that wife of yours right and proper! What's that?! Ain't got business with me, eh? Well, you may not have any with me, but I've got plenty of business with you! So open up this confounded door, you rascal! I'm coming in!"

Akechi seemed to have gone out to the porch to deal with the man, but his words were drowned out by the vagrant's cries.

Hearing the commotion, the beggar on the road sprinted closer, glancing around before creeping through the stone gate himself and watching the scene from the shadow of a lamppost. What he saw was Akechi Kogorō standing defiantly before the vagrant, who had one foot on the porch's stone steps. He was shrieking wildly, waving his fists in front of the detective's face.

Akechi was not a bit fazed and stared at the man in silence. Then, as if he could stand the escalating verbal abuse no longer, he cried out, "Fool! If I said I've got no business with you, then I've got no business! Now get out!" Then he pushed the stranger away.

The dirty man staggered back, but caught himself again. Howling gibberish, he grappled with Akechi.

No matter how wild he may have been, there was no way this man could overpower three-dan judo master Akechi. The assailant's arm was instantly twisted back, and he went crashing down onto the paved stones beyond the porch. Stunned, the man couldn't move for a moment out of sheer pain, but then he got to his feet again. But by the time he did, the front door was already shut tight, and Akechi was nowhere to be seen.

The stranger went to the porch and tried opening the door, but it seemed to be locked from the inside and wouldn't budge.

"Coward! You'd better remember this!" Finally, he gave up, muttering curse after curse as he went out to the gate.

The beggar, who had seen everything, let the stranger pass by and then followed him stealthily. Once they were removed a short distance from the Akechi estate, the beggar called out to him.

"'Scuse me," he said.

"Eh?" The raggedy man turned around to the filthy beggar in surprise. "What, a hobo? Sorry, I ain't rich enough to hand money out to people," he spat out and moved to leave.

"That's not why I stopped you. There's something I want to ask you."

"What's that?"

The beggar's tone was a bit unusual, so the dirty man peered into his face suspiciously.

"Despite my appearance, I'm not really a beggar. As a matter of fact, I work for Twenty Faces, and I've been spying on that pesky Akechi since yesterday. Looks like you bear quite a grudge against him."

So the beggar *was* one of Twenty Faces' henchmen after all.

"Bear a grudge? I was thrown in the slammer because of that rotten detective! And I'm gonna get my revenge come hell or high water!" The man flailed his fists around in rage.

"What's your name?"

"Akai Torazō."

"Who do you work for?"

"Ain't got no boss. I work alone."

"Hmph. Is that so?" The beggar thought for a moment. Then, as if he had thought of something, he abruptly changed the subject. "Have you heard of my boss, Twenty Faces?"

"What do you think I am, a dummy? He's a real talented guy."

"It's not just talent. He's a real magician. He's planning to loot the national museum next, you know. Your friend Akechi Kogorō is my boss's enemy, and that means we're on the same side. How about coming to work for Twenty Faces? If you do, believe me, you'll get your revenge soon enough."

Akai Torazō took a long, hard look at the beggar, then clapped his hands together. "Okay, I've made up my mind. Introduce me to this boss of yours!" he said, eager to join the band.

"Sure. If you hate Akechi that much, then I'm sure he'll be pleased. Before that, though, how about doing a little work to show your loyalty? It's time to kidnap that crummy detective." Twenty Faces' henchman lowered his voice as he spoke, shifting his gaze to and fro.

25 THE MASTER DETECTIVE, IN DISTRESS

"ARE YOU KIDDIN' ME? You're gonna kidnap that rat? Now that sounds like fun! I hadn't even dreamed of something like that! Hey, will you let me help out? I'd love to lend a hand! Just when are you gonna go about it anyways?" Akai Torazō asked eagerly.

"Tonight."

"T-t-tonight?! Well, ain't you in a hurry! But how're you gonna do it?"

"Hey, Twenty Faces is my boss, remember? He's already got a pretty clever plan. Here's the idea: we're gonna fix up one of the girls, a real looker, like someone's wife, and send her over there to ask for that bonehead's help on some kinda complicated job he would really go for.

"Then she's gonna ask him to come search her house and put him in a cab. Together with her, see? And obviously the driver's gonna be one of ours, too.

"Anyway, that knucklehead loves hard cases, right? And plus, his client this time is some damsel in distress, so he's bound to let his guard down and fall right into our trap.

"Now, what we've gotta do is go on ahead to the Aoyama Cemetery, then wait for the car with Akechi in it to arrive. Their route's gonna send them along that road.

"Once they're in front of us, the car will come to a complete stop. Then you and I are gonna open the doors from either side, jump in, and make it so the sucker can't move. Then we hit him with the anesthetic. I've got it right here in my pocket.

There'll also be two pistols. The other group will be carrying one. But they don't matter—it's not like they have some personal vendetta against Akechi. That's why I want you to come along. Now here's the pistol." The disguised man pulled a gun out of his frayed pocket and handed it to Akai.

"I've never fired one of these before. What do I do?"

"Aw, relax, it's empty. All you gotta do is put your finger on the trigger and make it look like you're gonna shoot. Twenty Faces hates poppin' people, you know. The pistol's just for scares."

Hearing that there were no bullets in the gun, Akai looked a bit disappointed but stuck it in his pocket regardless. "Guess we should head off to the cemetery then," he suggested.

"Nah, it's still a little early for that. We're supposed to start at seven, or maybe even a little later. The point is, we've still got two hours. Let's take it easy and go grab a bite to eat somewhere," the beggar said. Unwrapping the filthy bundle he had under one arm, the henchman pulled out a cloak and put it on over his grimy kimono.

The two dined at a cheap restaurant nearby. By the time they reached the Aoyama Cemetery, the sun had already gone down, and aside from the sparse streetlights, the area was pitch black. The place was so desolate it seemed like a wraith might appear at any minute.

The designated spot was on a tiny back road deep behind the graves, a dark area that cars seldom passed through at night. The two men sat down in the blackness, waiting for the car to arrive.

"They're sure taking their sweet time. I feel like I'm gonna freeze my butt off sitting out here."

"It'll be any moment now. When I looked at the clock on that store in front of the cemetery, it was 7:20. We've been here for more than ten minutes, so they should come soon."

The men waited for another ten minutes, talking off and on, when they were blinded by the headlights of an oncoming car.

"Hey, they're here. That's them. It has to be them. Get ready!"

Just as planned, the car screeched to a stop when it reached the duo.

"Now!" The men instantly jumped out from the dark.

"You take that side!"

"All right!"

Two black shadows sandwiched the car. Yanking open the doors, they each pointed a pistol at the person sitting inside. Simultaneously, a woman in western clothes sitting in the passenger side pulled out a pistol. At this point, even the driver had turned around and brandished his own pistol, which gleamed in the moonlight. Four pistol barrels were aimed at the lone person sitting in the back.

And of course, that person was Akechi Kogorō. Just as Twenty Faces had anticipated, the detective had been caught in the sinister plot. Or had he?

"Don't try anything funny or we'll shoot!" someone shouted menacingly.

As if resigned to his fate, Akechi remained completely still and made no attempt to resist. He was so docile, in fact, that even the thieves thought it eerie.

"Get him!" a low but strong voice echoed, and the man dressed as a beggar and Akai Torazō practically leaped into the car. While Akai held Akechi's upper body down, his partner pulled out a clump of white cloth from his pocket and hurriedly covered the detective's mouth. After a short while, the man's body relaxed. When the thief removed his hand five minutes later, it was clear that even the master detective was helpless against the drug. He was unconscious, as limp as a corpse.

"Ha! What a pushover," laughed the woman in western clothing in her beautiful voice.

"Hey, don't forget the rope. Bring it out here."

The beggar took a coil of rope from the driver, and Akai helped him bind Akechi's hands and legs. Now he wouldn't be able to move even if he did wake up.

"There we go. This master detective's as harmless as a pussy-cat now! This job's as good as done. Hey, the boss is waiting, isn't he? Let's hurry."

Akechi's trussed-up body was rolled onto the floor of the car, the thieves piled in, and the vehicle sped off. Their destination, of course, was Twenty Faces' lair.

26 LAIR OF THE FIEND

THE CAR CARRYING THE beautiful woman, the beggar, Akai Torazō, and the unconscious Akechi Kogorō sped along deserted streets. Finally, it passed the Meiji Shrine in Yoyogi and stopped in front of the gate to a house nestled within a dark copse. It was a middle-class home with seven or eight rooms, and the nameplate on the gatepost read Kitagawa Jūrō. Perhaps the occupants inside were asleep, but there was no light in any windows of the seemingly modest family's house.

The toady disguised as the driver got out of the car first and rang the bell on the gate. Almost immediately, a small peephole in the gate snapped open revealing two big eyes. They blazed intensely in the glow of the gate's lantern.

"Oh, it's you. How did it go? Did you get him?" the owner of the eyeballs whispered in a low voice.

"Yes, we got him, all right. Open up!" the driver demanded, and the doors of the gate began to creak. Behind the gate, a black-clad flunky was vigilantly guarding the entrance.

The beggar and Akai Torazō lifted detective Akechi's limp body. With the beautiful woman helping them, they disappeared inside, and the gate swung shut as if nothing had happened.

The driver jumped back into the empty car and sped off into the night. The villain's garage was most likely located elsewhere.

The trio approached the lattice door at the entrance to the house. An electric light at the front of the house snapped on. It was blindingly bright. Akai Torazō was startled by the brilliant illumination—but that was merely the beginning of his astonishment. Just after the light went on, a loud voice boomed out from regions unknown. No one had appeared; the voice simply floated through the air like a disembodied specter.

"Your numbers seem to have grown by one. Who is that?" The voice echoed strangely, as if it were not human.

Looking a bit uncomfortable, the newcomer Akai nervously scanned his surroundings. As he did, the subordinate dressed like a beggar walked briskly over to one of the pillars of the entrance and put his mouth to it.

"He's a new accomplice, a guy who has a serious grudge against Akechi. We can trust him," he said, as if speaking into a phone.

"Is that so? Well then, come inside," echoed the strange voice, and the lattice door mechanically slid open.

"Heh heh. Surprised? That was the boss, who's all the way in the back. In order to keep himself hidden, he has an amplifier and a microphone in this pillar. He's got to be careful after all," the beggar explained.

"How did he know I'm here, though?" Akai was still leery.

"You'll soon find out," the beggar said as he carried Akai further into the house. Akai followed.

In the entryway, another strong-looking man stood attentively. When he saw the group, he smiled and nodded. Opening a screen door, they entered a hall and walked down to the last room. Oddly enough, what they found was an empty fourteen-square-meter room.

The beggar motioned with his chin, and the beautiful woman clacked toward an alcove in the room to press on the back of the wall. As soon as she did, a boom followed by a heavy rumbling was heard. The tatami mats in the center of the room dropped straight down, revealing a black, rectangular hole.

"All right, now climb down these steps," Akai was told. He peered into the hole, and sure enough, sturdy wooden stairs led downwards.

Oh, what prudence! This way, even if someone made it past both the checkpoints at the gate and the front entrance, as long as they didn't know to lift the tatami mats, they would never figure out where Twenty Faces was.

"What are you standing around for? Hurry it up!"

Carrying Akechi's body, the trio descended the stairs. Once they were at the bottom, a mechanical drone whined above their heads, and the hole was once again sealed. It was truly a device of genius! But this basement room still wasn't where the boss was lurking. Guided by dim lights, the three criminals crept through a concrete hallway until their path was blocked by an iron door.

The man disguised as a beggar rapped on the door in an unusual rhythm. When he had finished, the heavy doors slid inwards, and blinding electric light illuminated an extravagant western-style room with dazzlingly beautiful furnishings. Smiling and sitting in an easy chair in the front was a well-dressed man who appeared to be around thirty years old—Twenty Faces in the flesh. No one knew if this was his real face, but he was a good-looking, clean-shaven man with curly hair.

"Well done, well done. Your service shall not be forgotten."

Naturally, the boss looked ecstatic now that he had imprisoned his archenemy Akechi Kogorō. As long as Twenty Faces could keep Akechi confined like this, no fearsome opponent stood between him and the treasures of Japan. Poor detective Akechi was rolled onto the floor, still bound. Unsatisfied with simply dropping him, Akai Torazō also kicked the unconscious detective in the head a few times.

"Ah, it seems like you really do bear hatred toward this man. That makes us allies. But that's enough. Enemies are to be taken care of, and besides, this man is the only master detective that Japan's got. Stop being so barbaric. Untie the fellow, and lay him down on that sofa." Like any good boss, Twenty Faces knew exactly how to treat his captives.

His underlings untied the detective and set him on the sofa as they were ordered, but the effects of the drug still hadn't worn off, so he remained slumped in unconsciousness.

The beggar described the details of Akechi's kidnapping and why he chose to recruit Akai Torazō.

"Yes, excellent work. It looks like you'll be a very useful fellow to have around, Akai. And I love the fact that you bear a grudge against Akechi." The joy of capturing the master detective had invigorated Twenty Faces.

Akai pledged his allegiance to Twenty Faces once more then asked something that had been puzzling him since he arrived. "All these gadgets really surprise me. With stuff like that, I guess we don't even hafta worry about the cops. One thing still hasn't fallen into place for me, though. When we were at the entrance, how'd ya see us like that?"

"Ha ha ha. Oh, that? If you want to know about that, look inside here." The boss pointed to a chimney-like pipe extending from a corner of the ceiling. As directed, Akai put his eye to the bent tube on the end. And what did he see? It was as if a picture of the entranceway had been shrunk and projected inside the tube. He could also clearly see the gatekeeper, still standing dutifully at his post.

"It's a periscope just like the ones they use in submarines. This one has a few more bends, though." So that's why such a powerful light was necessary. "But you haven't seen even half the devices in this house. There are some that only I know about. This is my stronghold. I have many other hideouts, but they're little more than temporary residences for deceiving the enemy." The rundown house in Toyamagahara where Kobayashi was imprisoned must have been one of those. "Someday I might even show you the art chamber beyond this room."

Twenty Faces was still in the clouds, his words flooding out. Behind his easy chair, a complicated mechanism that resembled a bank vault door was securely shut.

"There are many rooms behind here. Ha ha ha. Surprised? This basement is far more spacious than the house above it. These halls contain my many spoils of war, categorized and displayed accordingly. I'll show you someday.

"There are also some rooms that still have nothing in them, but quite soon they'll be filled to the brim with national treasures. You've read about it in the papers too, haven't you? All those treasures from that national museum."

With his nemesis Akechi out of the way, Twenty Faces considered the works of art as good as his. The fiend laughed on and on, enraptured.

27   THE BOY DETECTIVES

WHEN AKECHI DIDN'T RETURN home the next morning, panic broke out in his household. They had written down the address of the lady who requested his help, but after contacting the residence, they learned that no such woman lived there. This was when everyone first realized that Akechi's disappearance was the work of Twenty Faces.

Numerous newspapers published red banner headlines reading "AKECHI KOGORŌ KIDNAPPED" in their evening editions along with large photos of the detective. The case was also described in detail on the radio.

"Our beloved master detective has become the prisoner of a thief! The national museum is in peril!"

The nine million residents of Tokyo lamented the man's capture as if they had lost a family member and gathered and spread rumors about the case. The capital was shrouded in dark clouds of anxiety.

But the one who felt the most chagrin about the master detective's kidnapping was Kobayashi Yoshio. He waited all night and through the next day, but by the following evening Akechi had still not returned. The police said he had been kidnapped by Twenty Faces, and the newspapers and radio repeated the report. Kobayashi wasn't simply worried about the safety of his teacher. He was furious at the way the master detective's name had been disgraced.

The task of consoling Mrs. Akechi also fell to Kobayashi. As the wife of a master detective, she would not allow herself to shed any tears, but instead forced a smile on her pale face, drained of its vitality by anxiety. She just couldn't bear the news.

"Don't worry, ma'am. Mr. Akechi would never let himself be taken prisoner by that thief! I'm sure he has some intricate plan prepared that we don't know about. That's why it's taking him so long to come home," Kobayashi said, consoling the woman. But he had no real faith in what he was saying, so as he continued speaking, the unrest in his own heart bubbled up and his voice cracked.

At this dire hour, Kobayashi Yoshio, the genius assistant detective, felt as if he were at the end of his rope. He had absolutely no clue where Twenty Faces' hideout was located.

Two days before, a thief had come to spy in the guise of a picture-card storyteller, so someone may have been lurking in the vicinity now as well. If there were, it would be his only hope of finding Twenty Faces' lair. Kobayashi ran to the second floor and looked out the front window, but saw no one suspicious. Perhaps, having done their kidnapping, there was no more need for such surveillance.

And so, Kobayashi's second night of unrest ended, and the third morning came. It was Sunday. Mrs. Akechi and Kobayashi had just finished a lonely breakfast when all of a sudden, a boy shot toward the front door like a bullet.

"Excuse me! Is Kobayashi here? My name is Hashiba."

Hearing the loud voice, Kobayashi looked out to discover none other than Hashiba Sōji. The boy's cute little face was red, and he was out of breath. He must have been running. Now, surely you have not forgotten this character, Intrepid Reader. He was the son of the big businessman Hashiba Sōtarō, and had once set a trap in his home garden that caused Twenty Faces considerable pain and trouble.

"Is that you, Sōji? What a surprise. Come on in!" Sōji was two years younger than Kobayashi, who treated the boy much like a little brother as he led him into the parlor.

"What's the emergency?" he asked, only to hear the kid reply in a composed, adult voice.

"Mr. Akechi really got into some big trouble this time. You still don't know where he is, do you? That's what I came to talk to you about.

"Ever since the incident with my family, I've admired you. And I decided that I want to be just like you. I've told everyone at school about your great work and managed to find ten other kids who feel the same as me.

"We're going to create an association called the Boy Detectives. Of course, we're going to do it so that it won't interfere with our schoolwork. My dad also said that it's OK as long as it doesn't get in the way of school.

"Today's Sunday, you know? That's why I've brought everyone to your place. I wonder if you'd allow us to join you, with you leading us, of course, in searching for Mr. Akechi." Saying it all in one breath, Sōji stared intently at Kobayashi with his young eyes, awaiting an answer.

"Thank you." Kobayashi felt like he was about to cry, but just barely managed to suppress his tears and gripped Sōji's hand. "I can't imagine how happy Mr. Akechi will be when he hears about this. Yes, by all means, help me out with your Boy Detectives! I'm sure we'll be able to find some kind of clue if we work together. You're all a bit different from me, so I won't let you do anything dangerous. I don't know what I'd say to your parents if something were to happen.

"What I'm thinking of now is a type of detective work that isn't the least bit dangerous. Have you heard the word 'legwork' before? It means going around and listening to what a bunch of different people have to say, letting not the tiniest detail slip by, to find some kind of clue.

"Now, we're quicker than the average adult, and people are more likely to drop their guards around us, so I'm sure this'll work out well. Also, I know what the woman who took Mr. Akechi away two nights ago was wearing, what she looked like, and which direction her car headed. So all we need to do is head in that direction and do some legwork.

"You can talk to young people in shops, policemen, mailmen, or even just the kids who play around there. The important thing is to keep asking questions. We may know the direction, but the streets branch off a lot so it'll be hard to narrow it down to the right one. Since we have a lot of people working together, though, we should be all right. Whenever the street splits, we'll just send someone down the new path. Hopefully, if we do legwork all day, we'll be able to come up with something."

"Yes, let's do it! That'll be a piece of cake. Do you mind if I call all the Boy Detectives inside the gate?"

"Sure, go ahead. I'll come outside with you."

And so, after asking Mrs. Akechi to make sure it was all right, Kobayashi went out to the porch with Sōji. At that point, the boy broke into a run, speeding outside the gate and coming back with ten other members behind him.

To Kobayashi, they all looked to be healthy, fit fifth and sixth graders. Sōji introduced each of them to Kobayashi from atop the porch, then explained the investigation down to the last detail.

"Hip, hip, hooray for Captain Kobayashi!"

The boy was immediately designated the leader, and some of the other kids were so happy that they began shouting in joy.

"Let's go!"

Like a troop of Boy Scouts, the little detectives lined up and disappeared through the gate.

THE BOY DETECTIVES' GALLANT search continued through Sunday, Monday, Tuesday, and Wednesday. But no matter how much of their free time after school they used, no matter how hard they persevered, and no matter how long they searched, they failed to find a definitive clue.

But this was a case so difficult that not even thousands of Tokyo police could crack it. Just because they hadn't found a clue didn't mean the boys' search team was inefficient. And there was no telling what clues they might find in the remaining days.

With detective Akechi's whereabouts still unknown, the dreaded date of December 10 drew ever nearer. The Metropolitan Police Department had grown agonizingly impatient. After all, the target was national treasures this time! The chief of detectives, as well as Chief Inspector Nakamura, who had played a direct part in the Twenty Faces case, seemed on the verge of mental breakdowns.

But two days before the date, on December 8, another incident happened that sent the public wild. On that day, a letter to the editor written by Twenty Faces himself was published in the local news section of the *Mainichi Daily News*.

This newspaper wasn't controlled by the thief, but there was no way they could avoid printing a letter from Twenty Faces, the very wellspring of chaos in the city. An editorial meeting was held, and in the end, they decided to print the entire thing:

> I announced the date of my visit to the national museum as December 10, but feeling that it would be more chivalrous

> to make a more precise pledge, I would like to announce the time to all the citizens of Tokyo. It will be 4:00 p.m. on December 10. I invite the curator of the museum and the superintendent general of the police to take all due precautions. The more rigorous the guard, the greater my adventure shall shine.

Oh, what gall! He not only announced the date but had the audacity to publicly announce the time of his arrival as well. And he went so far as to blatantly insult both the museum curator and the entire Metropolitan Police Department.

I should not have to describe the shock that rippled through the people of Tokyo when they read it. Even those who had been laughing at such a ridiculous scenario finally lost their smiles.

The current curator of the museum was a doctor of literature named Kitakōji, an eminent historical scholar. Even this elderly academic was now forced to take the thief's announcement seriously. He went all the way out to the Metropolitan Police Department to learn about the security measures they would be taking and had a lengthy discussion with the superintendent general.

But that wasn't all. The news about Twenty Faces had become a topic of cabinet meetings with government ministers. The prime minister and the minister of justice were both so worried, in fact, that they called the superintendent general into a separate room and encouraged him to make a greater effort.

Days of unease for the people of Tokyo continued, until the tenth finally came.

Dr. Kitakōji had been at the national museum since early that morning, along with his three chief clerks, ten secretaries, fifteen security guards, and custodians. Every last person had been ordered to come in for work and report to a separate guard station.

Naturally they had closed the museum and locked the front gate.

From the Metropolitan Police Department, a group of fifty policemen hand-picked and led by Chief Inspector Nakamura arrived on the scene. Circling the walls and both gates, they picked out important points on the grounds: not even an ant could squeeze through their guard.

At 3:30 p.m., with no more than thirty minutes left until the appointed time, the policemen were dead serious. A large truck from the MPD arrived on the scene, carrying the superintendent general and the chief of detectives. The superintendent general was so worried that he couldn't sit still. He couldn't bear this pulse-pounding situation without keeping an eye on the museum personally. After inspecting the guard kept by their subordinates, the superintendent general and the others entered the museum to speak with Dr. Kitakōji.

"I didn't think you would grace us with your presence today, sir. I'm honored." Dr. Kitakōji welcomed the men, and the superintendent general responded with a slightly bashful smile.

"I'm embarrassed to say it, but I just couldn't stay still at a time like this. It's truly shameful that we have to amass such a force in order to deal with some measly little robber. Since the moment I joined the police force, we've never received an insult of this degree."

Dr. Kitakōji laughed weakly. "I feel the same way. I've been battling insomnia for the past week all because of some two-bit cat burglar!"

"But we only have twenty more minutes left now. Mr. Kitakōji, wouldn't you agree that no matter how much of a magician that man is, getting through our regiment and stealing all those art pieces in the scope of twenty minutes is a bit too tall an order?"

"I'm not sure. I know nothing about magicians, you see. I just wish four o'clock would hurry up and pass already." The historian seemed a bit angry. All this talk about Twenty Faces must have been irritating him.

The three men in the room said no more after that, each of them silently staring at the clock on the wall. The burly superintendent general clad in his gold-braided uniform, the chief of detectives, with his medium build and finely trimmed mustache, and the white-haired Dr. Kitakōji, his stick-thin figure clad in a business suit. The sight of these men sitting in their easy chairs and constantly glancing at the steadily ticking hands of the clock was far from dignified and seemed more bizarre than anything else. They passed ten minutes like this until the chief of detectives could bear the silence no longer and suddenly said, "I wonder what Akechi's up to? I know him personally, so this recent development truly puzzles me. Judging from the work he's done so far, such a grave slip-up would be unthinkable."

The superintendent general turned and stared at his subordinate. "I know you and your men worship that fellow, with your 'Akechi this and Akechi that' as if he were some sort of crime-solving god, but I don't buy it one bit. No matter how skilled he may be, he's still just one private detective. What can he do? From what I hear, he was talking about capturing Twenty Faces himself. How conceited! This failure of his should turn out to be some good medicine."

"Yes, but considering all of Akechi's achievements so far, I'm not sure that's all that can be said about this. I was just talking to Nakamura outside, and I think it would have helped us to have that man at our side right now," the chief of detectives said.

Just then the door to the office opened, and a person appeared.

"Akechi *is* at your side," he said with a smile.

"Akechi!" The chief of detectives leaped up from his chair.

Clad in a neat black suit with his hair unkempt as always, it was indeed Akechi Kogorō.

"Akechi, why are you—"

"I'll explain that later. For now, there's something more important we need to talk about."

"Of course—we must protect the art from being stolen."

"No, I'm afraid it's too late for that. See for yourselves. The appointed time has already come and gone."

The superintendent general, chief of detectives, and curator all looked at the electric clock on the wall. Sure enough, the minute hand had already passed the number twelve.

"Wait a minute, then that means Twenty Faces lied! There hasn't been a single disturbance in the. . ."

"That's right. It's already past four o'clock. It looks like he wasn't able to do anything after all!" the chief of detectives said triumphantly.

"No, the thief kept his promise," Akechi said gravely. "This museum is as good as empty."

29 The Master Detective's Rampage

"Wh-what? What did you say just now? Not a thing has been stolen! I just went around checking the exhibitions myself a few minutes ago! There are also fifty policemen stationed around the museum, and they aren't blind, you know!" the disbelieving superintendent general barked at Akechi.

"And yet everything has been stolen. Twenty Faces used a little of that magic he has been known to deal in. If you'd like, please come with me and see for yourselves," Akechi said quietly.

"Hmph! So you say everything's stolen, huh? Fine then, let's all go look together. Dr. Kitakōji, please come with us to the displays and see if this man's telling the truth." Doubting that Akechi would lie, the superintendent general decided to go and check.

"All right, then. Right this way, doctor." Akechi nodded, smiling at the white-haired scholar.

The four men left the office and walked down a corridor to the main display halls. There Akechi kindly took the hand of the elderly Dr. Kitakōji and led him to the front.

"Akechi, are you sure you didn't just doze off and have a daydream or something? There's nothing amiss here!" the chief of detectives shouted as they entered the hall.

Just as he claimed, all of the nation's statues were lined up neatly in their glass cases. There wasn't a single one missing.

"These?" Akechi pointed to the statues, looking meaningfully back at the chief of detectives, and then calling out to one of the security guards standing nearby. "Can you open this glass door for me?"

The security guard didn't know who Akechi was, but since he was with the curator and the superintendent general, he obeyed. A key was brought at once, and the large glass case was opened.

Then Akechi did something truly inexplicable.

What had possessed him? He reached into the case and snapped off one of the splendid-looking arms of the biggest ancient wooden statue! The other three men were too dumb-founded by the suddenness of the detective's actions to stop him. And so, Akechi went on through the entire shelf, ripping limb after limb off the five national masterpieces. Some had their arms removed, others had their heads ripped off, and still others lost entire fingers. It was an atrocious sight.

"Akechi, what are you doing? Hey, don't let him do that! Stop!" The superintendent general and the chief of detectives both shouted at Akechi, who quickly hopped back from the case, returned to the curator's side, took his hand once more and smiled.

"Hey, Akechi! What's gotten into you? There's a limit to how reckless you can be with your inspections, you know! These are the most valued pieces of art in the entire museum!" The chief of detectives looked as if he were going to grapple with the inspector at any minute.

"These? National treasures? Maybe you should have your eyes checked. Come on, look closely now. Examine the damage I just did to the statues." Taken aback by the confidence in the man's voice, the officer approached the statues and peered into the gaping holes.

And what did he find beneath the holes where heads and arms once were but fresh white wood that scarcely matched the blackened, ancient wood around them! There was no pos-sible way a sculpture from the Nara period, more than a thou-sand years before, could be made of brand-new materials!

"Are you saying that these statues are fakes?"

"Indeed. If you fellows had better eyes for art, you wouldn't even have to look into the holes to tell that all of these are fakes. The perpetrator created imitations with new materials then painted them to make them look older. If you passed these on to a forgery specialist, he'd say the same thing," Akechi explained nonchalantly.

"Just *what* is the meaning of this, Dr. Kitakōji? How could all the pieces in this museum be fakes?" the superintendent general asked the curator, ready to rebuke him.

"I'm shocked. Positively shocked!" The old scholar stood frozen as he gripped Akechi's hand, mortified and beginning to panic.

Hearing the commotion, three other people ran to the scene. Among them was a specialist in ancient art who was working in this section as a chief clerk. The moment he looked at the broken statues, he instantly realized what had happened.

"Ah! These are all fakes! But that's strange—the real ones were here yesterday. I walked through the cases myself, so I'm positive of it."

"Which means that the real ones that were here yesterday were suddenly switched with the fake ones today. This doesn't make sense. What happened?" The superintendent general stared at the others in bewilderment.

"Still don't understand? The museum has been emptied out," Akechi said, pointing to another display case.

"Wh-what? Then that means you—" The chief of detectives was frantic.

Whether they understood the meaning of Akechi's words or not, the personnel in front shot over to the case and pressed their faces to the glass. They peered at the darkened Buddhist paintings and cried out in unison, "Ah! This one, this one, that one, they're all. . . Dr. Kitakōji! All these paintings are fakes! Every single one of them!"

"Go and check the other displays. Hurry, hurry!"

Without waiting for the chief's words, the three dashed from case to case like madmen, shouting and carrying on. "Fakes! All of these valuable treasures have been replaced by fakes!"

They nearly tumbled down the stairs to the next display hall and then quickly returned to the second floor. By then their numbers had grown to ten, every face red in anger.

"It's the same downstairs. The only real ones left are worthless. Every single valuable item has been replaced by an imitation. Dr. Kitakōji, we just talked with the others, and there doesn't seem to have been any disturbance. There wasn't a single fake here yesterday. Every single one of us is absolutely confident about his own pieces! In just a single day, roughly a hundred works of art were replaced with forgeries, like magic!" the employees of the museum shouted, nearly stamping the floor in outrage.

"Looks like that fiend outwitted us yet again, Akechi." The superintendent general looked back at Akechi pensively.

"Yes, he did. That thief robbed us blind, just like he said he would."

Out of all those present, Akechi was the only one who looked not a bit distracted and was even still smiling a bit. As if to encourage the curator, who seemed to have lost even the strength to cry out with shock, Akechi firmly gripped the old man's hand.

30　Secrets Revealed

"I still can't quite wrap my head around this, though. How is it humanly possible to remove that many pieces of art and replace them with fakes, all in the course of one day? Well, the fakes themselves were probably created ahead of time by people coming in here disguised as ordinary patrons and then drawing copies. It's the switch that's the problem. We just can't think of any way it could have been done!" The employees were all scratching their heads, as if stumped by a devilish mathematics problem.

"The real ones were all here until last night, correct?" the superintendent general asked the men.

"Yes, you can be sure of that," they all answered.

"Which means that at some point last night, some of Twenty Faces' henchmen must have sneaked in here."

"That's absolutely out of the question. The front gate, back gate, and walls were patrolled by a large number of policemen all night long. And the curator stayed overnight along with three other employees. How could they have transported all those valuables past such strict surveillance? It's absolutely impossible," the personnel said.

"I don't get it. This is truly strange. But it looks like Twenty Faces isn't quite the man he claimed to be. If he really replaced all of these works of art with fakes, then his announced time of four o'clock on December tenth meant nothing!" The chief of detectives could not restrain himself any longer and was now in a fury.

"And yet it was very meaningful," Akechi Kogorō said, defending Twenty Faces. He had had his hand wrapped tightly around Dr. Kitakōji's for some time now, as if the two were dear friends.

"Oh, it was very meaningful, now, was it? Then just what did it mean?" the superintendent general asked the master detective curiously.

"Take a look at that." Akechi neared a window and pointed to the open space behind the museum. "The reason why he had to wait until December tenth is right there."

On the lot was an old building that had been built as a night duty room when the museum was first constructed. It was no longer in use and demolition work had begun a few days before. By the tenth, the building had been completely torn down, and old pieces of wood and fragments of roof tiles lay strewn about.

"Yes, they tore down that old building. But what does that have to do with the Twenty Faces incident?" the other asked.

"You'll soon understand. I realize it may be a bit troubling, but could someone go to Chief Inspector Nakamura and tell him to send up the man who was scheduled to watch the back gate at noon today?"

Thoroughly confused as to what was going on, one of the museum employees heeded Akechi and hurried down the stairs. Soon Chief Inspector Nakamura appeared with a single policeman.

"Were you in charge of the back gate today?" Akechi asked.

Seeing the superintendent general, the policeman stood rigidly at attention and answered that he was.

"Then you saw a truck drive out between twelve and one."

"Yes, sir. I believe you're asking about the truck carrying the old wood that was torn down from that building, correct?"

"That's right."

"Then yes sir, it did pass through." The man's expression seemed to question why the old wood was so important.

"Have you all realized now? That's the secret to the thief's magic. While on the exterior, the truck seemed to be carrying nothing but old wood, it was actually filled with every single piece of artwork stolen from this museum." Akechi looked around as he revealed this shocking secret.

"Are you saying that the thief's minions were among the carpenters?" Chief Inspector Nakamura blinked repeatedly.

"Exactly. But there weren't just some among them. Every single one of those carpenters worked for the thief. Twenty Faces prepared things from quite early on and then waited for the perfect opportunity. The demolition of that old house began on the fifth, I believe. The date they were to start was decided on and announced to everyone involved three or four months before the fact. That way, they could plan to finish up and haul out all the wood on the tenth. That's how Twenty Faces calculated the date of his attack, and four o'clock was set to be the time when the art would all be safely in the thief's lair so that in case anyone was clued in to the fakes, it would already be too late. *That's* the meaning behind the time."

Oh, what a thorough plan! No matter the situation Twenty Faces' magic is always one step ahead of the imagination of the average man!

"But, Akechi, even if they transported it out that way, that still doesn't tell us how the thief entered the display halls and when he switched out all the art!" The chief of detectives couldn't bring himself to believe what he'd heard.

"The switch happened late last night," Akechi explained, as if he had everything figured out. "Each day the thief's underlings came here to work, they would bring a few of the imitations with them. Pictures were rolled up tightly, and statues were disassembled, with arms, legs, heads, and torsos each wrapped up separately. That way, if they were carried in like carpentry tools, no one would bat an eye. Everyone was so busy worrying about something getting stolen that they paid no attention to things being brought in. Then all the counterfeits were hidden under that mountain of old wood and brought in at night."

"But who changed them in the displays? All the carpenters went home last night. And even if a few remained inside, how could they get into the display halls? The entrances and exits were closed all night. Only the curator and three other people were here, watching closely without getting a wink of sleep. It's unthinkable that such a great number of pieces could have been switched without them noticing." The employee had posed a good question.

"That was accomplished by a truly daring method the thief had planned. The three employees who stayed here last night all went home in the morning, didn't they? Please call one of them and see if they are indeed home."

Akechi had once again confounded his audience. No one knew the phone numbers to any of the three men's homes, but they did have the phone numbers to stores near each of the three addresses. One employee picked up the phone at once, then systematically checked to see whether the three men had returned home in the morning. All of the men's wives replied that due to the nature of the case, they simply figured their husbands had had to stay on watch.

"It's now been roughly nine hours since those three left the museum, and yet they still haven't returned home. Don't you find that a bit strange? The three stayed up all last night working, so it's hard to imagine they went out frolicking somewhere. Now, gentlemen, can any of you guess why none of those men arrived at their homes?"

Akechi passed his eyes over the group once more, and then answered himself. "There is but one answer: because all three men were kidnapped by Twenty Faces' subordinates."

"What? Kidnapped? But when?" one employee shouted.

"Last night, when each of them left their homes to come to work."

"L-l-last night? But then, who were the three. . ."

"Twenty Faces' henchmen. The real three were imprisoned in the thief's lair while three of *his* men came here instead. It's quite a simple plan. Since the men on guard duty were thieves themselves, switching out all the art was like stealing candy from a baby. This is how Twenty Faces operates. With just a little clever thinking, he easily accomplishes these seemingly impossible feats." Detective Akechi complimented the villain while maintaining his vice-like grip on Dr. Kitakōji's wrist.

"Those men were working for the thief? How careless of me. I was so stupid!" The scholar shook his head and groaned in mortification. His eyes bulged and his face turned blue, making for a horrific visage of pure rage. Why hadn't he been able to figure out that his three employees were actually thieves in disguise? If it was Twenty Faces in disguise, the doctor's ignorance may have been understandable, but there's no way three mere underlings could have disguised themselves that well. Don't you find it strange, Intrepid Reader, that a man as intelligent as Dr. Kitakōji had been duped so easily?

31   TO CATCH A FIEND

"HOLD ON A MINUTE, Akechi," the superintendent general called out as if he had been waiting eagerly for the detective to finish speaking. "You explained the theft in such detail it's almost as if you're Twenty Faces in disguise. This couldn't just all be a result of your own deduction skills. Do you have any solid proof?"

"Obviously, this is not simply a product of my imagination. You see, I heard about all of the secrets from one of Twenty Faces' followers right before I came here, in fact."

"Wh-what? What's that? You met up with one of Twenty Faces' men? But where? How?" Even the superintendent general was dumbfounded by this twist.

"I met him at Twenty Faces' hideout. You heard that I was kidnapped by the thief, correct, sir? My family and the general populace believed the same, and it was also in the newspaper. But the truth is that was all part of my plan. I wasn't kidnapped at all. On the contrary, I myself became an ally of the thief and assisted him in the abduction of a certain man.

"Last year, I was approached by a stranger about an apprenticeship. When I saw him, I was shocked. It was as if someone had hung a mirror in front of my eyes. He looked exactly like me, right down to the last hair on his head. You see, the reason this man came to me was because he wanted to work as my body double, to be used as a substitute when I needed one most.

"Without anyone's knowledge, I employed this fellow and had him live in a certain place that would prove helpful later.

"On the day of the abduction, I left my house and went to his hideout. There, I changed my clothes and had him return to my office before I did. After a while, I transformed into a vagrant known as Akai Torazō, and then returned to the Akechi office. Once there, I went up to the porch and staged a little fight with my double.

"An underling of the thief saw this and completely believed what he was seeing. He approached me afterwards, saying that if I truly hated Akechi that much, I should come work for Twenty Faces. And so, after assisting in the kidnapping of my double, I was finally able to enter the enemy's stronghold.

"But, you know, that rascal Twenty Faces is quite the vigilant man. Despite having already joined his cause, he kept me working on jobs inside the house, not letting me set a single foot outside. And of course, he told me nothing about the measures he was taking to rob the national museum.

"Then finally today came. I had decided to wait until noon. Sure enough, right at two o'clock, the entrance to the basement opened, and a bunch of thieves dressed as carpenters carrying priceless works of art came down. These were obviously the treasures stolen from the museum.

"While I was guarding the basement, I prepared some sake and food. Then, the men who had just come back joined me and the others for a celebration. These thieves, in their elation at having completed such a monumental job, became rowdy and began drinking themselves silly. After thirty minutes they began falling asleep, until all of the men were out cold.

"Why, you ask? Haven't you already figured it out? I took some anesthetic from Twenty Faces' medicine room and mixed it in with their drinks beforehand. Afterwards I left the hideout on my own, found some local policemen, and told them the story. Then I asked them to arrest Twenty Faces' men and secure the stolen goods in his basement.

"You should all be glad to know that we were able to recover every one of the stolen goods: all of the art from this museum as well as the treasures from poor Mr. Kusakabe's Castle. And we returned all of the items that Twenty Faces had stolen over the years to their rightful owners."

The men listened to Akechi's story as if he had hypnotized them. Yes, the master detective hadn't smirched his rightful title in the least! Just as he had boasted, Akechi had been able to find the villain's hideout, take back all the stolen goods, and arrest a multitude of criminals all by himself.

"Well done, Akechi, well done. Looks like I had been misjudging you until now. I deeply apologize." The superintendent general approached the master detective and shook his left hand.

Why his left hand, you ask? That's because Akechi's right hand was busy with something else: keeping a tight grip on the wrist of the museum's curator. It was indeed strange. Why did Akechi insist on holding the man's hand for so long?

"So then Twenty Faces himself drank the anesthetic too, I assume? You've been talking solely about his underlings. I don't remember hearing about the man himself." Chief Inspector Nakamura was suddenly worried. "I can't believe you'd let the ringleader get away, though."

"No, Twenty Faces did not return to the basement. I have captured him, however," Akechi answered with a smile, grinning broadly enough to attract the attention of a certain man.

"Well then, where is he? Where'd you capture him?" Nakamura asked impatiently. The superintendent general and the others stared at Akechi's face and awaited his reply.

"Here," Akechi answered calmly.

"Here? But where?"

"Right here." Just what was Akechi trying to say?

"I'm talking about Twenty Faces," the policeman rephrased his question in puzzlement.

"I'm talking about Twenty Faces, too," Akechi said.

"Stop answering like this is some sort of riddle! The men standing here right now are all people we know! Or are you saying that Twenty Faces is hiding among us in this room?"

"Why, yes I am. Shall I show you a little proof? Sorry to bother you all again, but I have four guests waiting below. Would you mind calling them?" It seemed Akechi wasn't quite out of surprises.

Another employee hurried downstairs. After a moment, footsteps were heard, and Akechi's four guests appeared. Utterly surprised by what they saw, many of the people present found themselves gasping in shock. An old, white-haired gentleman was at the front. He was clearly the educated historian, Dr. Kitakōji. Behind him stood the three museum employees who had been missing since the night before.

"I saved these four from Twenty Faces' hideout," Akechi explained.

Oh, what a startling development! Now there were two museum curators present.

One was the Dr. Kitakōji who had just come up the stairs, and the other was the Dr. Kitakōji who had been in Akechi's grip since the start.

From their clothes right down to their faces, the two curators looked exactly alike, even in the way they were glaring at each other.

"Gentlemen, do you now understand just how masterful a disguise artist Twenty Faces is?" Detective Akechi shouted. He took the hand of the old man that he had been holding until then and twisted violently backwards. As soon as the man fell to the ground, his white hair and mustache were ripped off, revealing jet-black hair and a young, smooth face. It was, of course, the one and only Twenty Faces.

"Excellent work, Twenty Faces. That must have been quite painful, I imagine. I mean, from the very beginning, you had to do your very best to grin and bear it as I revealed the secrets of your entire plan to everyone, right in front of your very eyes. And even if you tried to run, there was no way you would have been able to escape from such a large group of people with my hand gripping you like a handcuff since the start of your ordeal. Have you started to lose feeling in your wrist? Please excuse me. I think I may have indulged myself a little too much." Akechi offered sarcastic consolation as he stared down with pity at the silent Twenty Faces.

But if Twenty Faces was disguised as the curator, then why hadn't he fled sooner? His mission had been completed the night before, so if he had simply left with his three disguised employees, he would never have had to suffer such embarrassment.

You must remember, Intrepid Reader: this is Twenty Faces we're talking about. Staying behind to see the outcome of his adventures was one of his greatest delights. He clearly wanted to see with his own eyes the horror on the policemen's faces when they found out about the fake art.

If Akechi hadn't shown up, Twenty Faces surely would have had the fake curator catch on to the theft a little past four o'clock and then gleefully torment the others. Indeed, that would have been exactly the kind of adventure that excited Twenty Faces most. Unfortunately, he had gotten a little too caught up in his adventuring and ended up committing a fatal error.

Detective Akechi turned to the superintendent general. "Sir, I would like to hand over the Fiend with Twenty Faces," he said politely.

Every man present had been dumbfounded by the flabbergasting scene unfolding before their eyes and even forgot to praise the detective on his excellent work. They were simply frozen where they stood. Finally, as if he had woken up from a dream, Chief Inspector Nakamura went over to Twenty Faces and produced a set of handcuffs. With practiced hands, the officer quickly secured the thief's hands behind his back.

"I'm grateful to you, Akechi. Thanks to your hard work, I can finally put the real Twenty Faces behind bars, after all we've suffered. I couldn't be happier." Tears of gratitude filled the man's eyes. "Now then, I'm going to take him and surprise the other officers out front. C'mon, Twenty Faces, on your feet!"

The Chief Inspector pulled the thief up and saluted the other men before filing down the stairs with the other policemen.

Dozens of officers were gathered at the front gate to the museum. Once they saw Chief Inspector Nakamura appear from the entrance, the officers dashed over, scrambling to be the first to see Twenty Faces.

"Rejoice, men! Thanks to our friend Akechi, we've finally got him! This is the ringleader of it all, Twenty Faces!" he said with pride as he was hailed by his fellows.

Twenty Faces looked pathetic. Whether or not the villain had accepted that his luck had finally run out, he seemed to no longer possess the strength to smile that cocky smile of his and meekly hung his head in shame.

The officers formed a line with the thief in the center and left the gate. Beyond the gate was a forested park, and beyond that two police cars were visible.

"Hey, someone call one of those over here."

One officer gripped his baton and dashed over. The rest followed, charging ahead to the distant vehicle. They had been lulled into a false sense of security by the thief's docile appearance. Even Chief Inspector Nakamura was completely focused on the car now. Strangely enough, all eyes were off the criminal at that moment, and for him, it was the perfect chance. Twenty Faces gritted his teeth, summoned up all his strength, and ripped the end of the rope from Nakamura's grasp.

"Stop!" By the time the Chief Inspector knew what was going on, the villain was ten meters away, sprinting like a racehorse. Still tightly bound by the rope, he seemed ready to topple over at any minute as he leaped into the forest.

At the entrance to the forest, ten elementary-school children who seemed to be taking a walk had stopped and were gazing intently at the man. As Twenty Faces ran, he realized the children were in his way, but he had to pass them to escape to the forest.

They're just a bunch of little kids. The minute they see my scary face, they'll surely run off in fright! And if they don't, I'll just kick them out of the way!

The thief considered his options and charged determinedly toward the children. But things did not go as Twenty Faces had expected, for the children not only did not run, they screamed wildly and pounced on the thief themselves.

I'm sure you've realized it by now, Intrepid Reader, that those schoolchildren were none other than the Boy Detectives led by Kobayashi Yoshio. They had already finished patrolling around the museum and were waiting for a chance to be of service.

Kobayashi jumped first, heading like a bullet toward Twenty Faces. Then came Hashiba Sōji followed by his classmates. They all piled on the villain one after another, quickly knocking down the helpless foe.

"Oh, thank you! You boys are so brave!"

Chief Inspector Nakamura soon came running up and thanked the boys. Then, with the help of his men, the officer carefully walked Twenty Faces over to the police car, which had driven up next to them. Just then a gentleman dressed in a black suit came out of the gate. It was detective Akechi, running to the scene of the commotion. Setting eyes on his unscathed teacher, Kobayashi let out a cry of pleasant surprise and ran to the detective.

"Oh, Kobayashi!" Detective Akechi called to the sprinting boy, stretching out both arms and catching him. It was a beautiful scene. The teacher and his pupil had worked hard and captured the fiend. And so, realizing that they were both safe, they thanked each other for their perseverance.

The police standing by were moved by the touching scene and watched the two with smiling faces. Suddenly everyone threw their hands high into the air and young voices called out, "Hip-hip-hooray for Mr. Akechi! Hip-hip-hooray for Captain Kobayashi!"

About the translator

DAN LUFFEY HAS BEEN living and traveling around Japan for the past four years. He received formal education in Japanese literature and translation at UC Santa Barbara and Kyoto University, and recently received an MA from Kyoto University of Art & Design. A lover of surreal and pulp fiction, Dan is passionate and dedicated about introducing more fantastic and culturally relevant Japanese literature into the English language. Aside from literature in translation, Dan is also involved in video game localization, TV subtitling, independent TV and film production, and film festivals in Western Japan. Ever-submerged in Japanese subculture and kitsch, he's always looking to broaden his horizon with new creative projects.

ABOUT THE ARTIST

TIM SMITH 3 HAS done professional artwork for numerous high-profile entertainment companies over the years. His work can be seen in Marvel Comics, Archie Comics, Papercutz, and DC Comics. To view more of TS3's work, please visit junemoon.net/wordpress/, TS3.deviantart, or facebook.com/TS333. He is also on Twitter @TS3.

Made in the USA
Middletown, DE
13 August 2020